The ATTIC and The ARK

Elizabeth Lavers

The Attic and The Ark

Elizabeth Lavers

Published by Easy Balance Books, this book is produced entirely in the UK, is available to order from most book shops in the United Kingdom and is globally available via UK-based Internet book retailers.

ISBN: 978-1-7397781-3-2

Cover Design: Martin Shute in association with Jag Lall

Copy editor: Sue Croft

The text pages of this book are produced via an independent certification process that ensures the trees from which the paper is produced comes from well managed sources that exclude the risk of using illegally logged timber while leaving options to use post-consumer recycled paper as well.

DEDICATION

For Simon, with love

and much appreciation to my brother Martin
who created the book cover

Also by Elizabeth Lavers

The Holiday Dragon
ISBN: 97847397781-0-1

Poetry Books

. . . and there was Light
ISBN: 978-0-9572053-0-7

Digital Clock
ISBN: 978-0-9572053-2-1

The Sundial
ISBN: 978-0-9572053-8-3

1

Jonathan always enjoyed visiting his grandparents but when he had just finished having measles and was invited to stay with them, it was far more exciting than usual as they had moved into a new house in the country, a house Jonathan had never seen. It was also the first time Jonathan had stayed anywhere on his own without his sisters. His grandparents had moved only ten days before and his grandmother was still unpacking and sorting out, while his grandfather attacked the weeds that were choking the garden.

The house was lovely, Jonathan thought, small but somehow unexpected. The steep black wooden stairs came right down into the sitting room opposite the big fireplace. Upstairs the floors were hardly flat anywhere but sloped in every direction, which made even a quiet game of marbles much more fun than usual. The guest bathroom was downstairs and had a red carpet and windows divided into little diamond shapes. At first there had been another good thing about the bathroom, a singing tap which made a noise you could hear right through the house whenever anybody turned it on – but a man had come to mend it and now it was just like any other tap.

Jonathan helped his grandmother indoors sometimes and sometimes, too, when he was allowed, he lent his grandfather a hand in the garden. His grandfather loved gardening and his gardening tools were all neatly hung on pegs at the back of the garage. There were spades, rakes, the sharp garden fork, a sickle and a coil of black and green hose, just like a snake.

Jonathan's bedroom was small and the window was low down with a wide window-ledge you could sit on. Jonathan had had to promise not to open the window, because his grandmother was afraid he would fall out onto the stone path by the back door; but even with the window closed you could see for miles and miles across fields and woods, with houses and farms dotted here and there.

"This is a super house," said Jonathan when he had looked everywhere.

His grandmother looked at him doubtfully. "Well, I do hope you are going to like being here," she said. "I'm afraid we haven't got any toys for you to play with but at least there's lots of space for you to run about outside. I must see if there are any children you could ask to come and play."

Jonathan had been there three or four days now but it seemed there were no children of about his age in any of the cottages nearby. He was not used to being on his own and after lunch he wandered round the garden, thinking what good places there were to hide in if only there was somebody to come looking for him.

After a while the front doorbell rang in the house and through the open window he heard his grandmother talking to a visitor. Jonathan went to float a leaf on the water in the big rain barrel by the back door. If he blew hard, the leaf just twisted round and round but if he gave a long steady blow, it raced across the water and bumped into the side of the barrel. He had been doing this for a few minutes when his grandfather opened the back door.

"Ah, Jonathan, there you are. Your grandmother wants to speak to you. I'm going to have a go at that border."

He disappeared round the side of the house and Jonathan went inside. His grandmother's visitor was called Mrs Nelson. She looked quite old but she smiled nicely at Jonathan when she said hello, and did not say what a big boy he was.

"I came to ask your grandmother whether you would like to come and see some toys I have at my house," she said. "They aren't new ones but you might find something you would like to play with. There's a rocking horse and some other toys."

Jonathan felt rather shy. He looked at his grandmother.

"I shall be coming along in a few minutes myself, Jonathan," she said. "I must just finish tidying things into the cupboard in the kitchen now Grandpa has put up all those hooks for me."

"Well," thought Jonathan, "I suppose it would be nice to go out."

He wasn't really very keen on rocking horses. His little sister, Elizabeth, had one at home and you couldn't rock very hard on it because the metal frame began to squeak and it was much too small for him anyway.

"Your grandmother tells me you have just had measles," said Mrs Nelson, as they shut the gate behind them and set off down the road.

"Yes, the others have got it now," said Jonathan, "so I was

allowed to come on a holiday and nobody has seen Grandpa's house yet, except me. Not even Catherine."

"How old is Catherine?" asked Mrs Nelson

"Seven and a half. Nearly eight," said Jonathan.

"This is my house, just here on the corner," said Mrs Nelson.

It was a big house made of grey stone and there was a notice on the gate. One word began with V but was too long for Jonathan to spell out.

"What does that say?" he asked.

"It says 'The Vicarage'," said Mrs Nelson. "Come along inside. My boys are all grown up, of course, and even my grandchildren are getting very big now but I do keep some toys upstairs for when children come to see me. You come and have a look."

There was a grandfather clock at the bottom of the stairs, and the large white cat asleep in a chair next to it looked at them lazily as they passed. Jonathan followed Mrs Nelson upstairs and along the landing, past two or three doors. Mrs Nelson stopped and opened a door but to Jonathan's surprise, instead of a room there were more stairs, leading steeply upward.

"Gosh," said Jonathan, impressed. "Is this a cupboard?"

"Well, no, not quite a cupboard," said Mrs Nelson. "It's more of a … a secret staircase."

"Crumbs!" said Jonathan, very impressed indeed.

He looked up the stairs. They were narrow wooden stairs with no carpet and if you tilted your head right back you could see a window in the ceiling at the top.

"Come on, then, Jonathan, let's go up," said Mrs Nelson.

"You go first, there isn't enough room for two at a time."

Rather pink with excitement, Jonathan climbed up the steep wooden stairs and stood waiting at the top. The sunshine fell through the window in the ceiling to make a warm golden rug on the landing. There were two doors, one of which was half open. From behind it there came the drips and gurglings of a water-tank. Mrs Nelson opened the other door and in his eagerness Jonathan almost fell into the room.

"Oh dear, do be careful of that awful step, I should have remembered to tell you," said Mrs Nelson, for the room was down a step from the landing and he had to clutch at the door to steady himself. But Jonathan didn't mind. He liked secret staircases and steps where you expected level floor.

The room itself was very oddly shaped, with walls pushing inwards in some places and making sharp turns where you least expected. There were three small windows, one of them in a deep alcove that was like a tiny room on its own and the ceiling sloped four different ways and wasn't flat anywhere. Several chairs and a table were pushed together against a wall, and an old sewing-machine, a birdcage, and some large cardboard boxes full of books stood on the table. One of the chairs was broken, and another held a pile of very dusty old magazines. A large picture was leaning face to the wall and although the room had no carpet, a carpet was lying rolled up beside the picture, tied in two places with string. Mrs Nelson walked past all these interesting things towards the alcove with the window.

"Over here, Jonathan," she said. "Here's the toy-box, and there is the horse, in the corner."

Jonathan saw a big wooden box and standing next to it a large doll's house. Right in the corner, beneath the window, was a horse – but what a horse! Jonathan scrambled hastily past the toy-box to have a look. This was no silly little metal toy but a horse whose head was higher than Jonathan's own. Its paint was old and worn but it had a real mane and tail of white horse-hair, and a leather saddle and bridle. Instead of curved rockers it had a kind of long, heavy frame and its four hooves were about a foot from the floor. Jonathan gazed at it in admiration.

"Crumbs!" he said at last. "It's even got proper stirrups. Can I ride it?"

"Well, we'll have to move it out into the room properly first," said Mrs Nelson.

Between them they pushed the big toy-box a little way, then slid the horse out into the middle of the room. Jonathan reached up to the saddle, put one foot in an iron stirrup and tried to climb on to its back. At once the horse plunged forward, almost throwing him off, but Mrs Nelson caught it by the bridle and Jonathan managed to scramble into the saddle. He put both feet into the stirrups, picked up the worn leather reins and began to ride. The horse leapt right forward and rocked right back each time in a most exciting way and its mane tossed backwards and tangled into the reins as Jonathan rode. Everything in the attic went into a blur, except for the bright sunshine coming in the window, and just before Jonathan stopped rocking at last and let the horse come to a stop, he had almost forgotten where he was and was so out of breath that he could hardly speak.

"Gosh," he said at last. "Doesn't it go fast? It was really galloping!"

Mrs Nelson came and held the horse's head for him while he slid off.

"I hope you haven't got too dusty," she said. "He always was a lovely horse, though he's got rather shabby now. He could really do with a coat of paint and perhaps a drop of oil on his poor creaking joints. I must remember to talk to my husband about it. Now, let's just see if there is anything in the box you might like to play with. Oh, there's the doorbell, that must be your grandmother. I'll go and let her in and make a cup of tea, and you just rummage about and see what you can find."

Mrs Nelson disappeared down the stairs, and Jonathan was quite alone in the attic. The dust danced in the sunlight coming in through a window and a bird was chirping quietly outside on the gutter. Jonathan looked at the toy-box. It came up past his middle and was covered over at the top with a sheet of brown paper which he pulled off and left on the floor. First he found a very small wheelbarrow and some skittles tied together with string, and a watering can which was wedged in amongst the toys and was rather difficult to pull out.

As he lifted these things out of the box, Jonathan put them carefully down on the floor, on the brown paper. There was a big bag full of hard lumpy shapes, which turned out to be wooden blocks, rather a good wooden engine with two trucks, and a round tin, the sort that you sometimes get biscuits in at Christmas-time, full of something that rattled but Jonathan could not get the lid off. After trying for a while, he put the tin down and drove the engine round the floor of the attic. He built a bridge for it out of the bricks. Then he went back to look in the box again. By now he had to hang over into the box, balancing on his tummy on the edge as he reached for more things to pull out. Another bag, with a drawstring at the top, felt very exciting but was only full of lots of furniture for the doll's house although there seemed to be something good underneath it. One of Jonathan's feet left the floor and waved wildly in the air as he tugged with both hands. The thing, whatever it was, moved a bit but it did not come right out. It seemed to be some kind of boat. At that moment, Jonathan heard his grandmother's voice calling him from downstairs.

"Just coming, Granny," he called back, then bent again into the box and gave one last pull. This time the boat came free. It was rather heavy but Jonathan got it out and turned with it to go downstairs, holding it against his chest. He was surprised to find that the patch of sunshine had moved from the head of the stairs and was now splashed against the wall. He went very carefully on the steep narrow stairs. The boat was big and wide with a wooden roof, and there seemed to be something inside which rattled as he put it down on the landing to shut the door to the secret staircase. Jonathan went on downstairs and found his grandmother and Mrs Nelson drinking tea in the room across the hall.

"Hello, Granny," said Jonathan. "Look at this boat. I think there's something inside, and there's lots of super things upstairs, everything you can think of, and the horse is enormous!"

"Oh, darling, how lovely," said his grandmother. "I'm glad you've had such a nice time. Let me see the boat. Oh, look, it's an Ark, a Noah's Ark."

"An Ark? Gosh, is it really?" said Jonathan, delighted, and looked at it properly for the first time. He loved the story of Noah and the Ark, and Catherine had a picture in one of her books of the animals hurrying two by two up the wide gangplank in the pouring rain. Sure enough, he was holding a Noah's Ark, and now he came to look, there was a little hook to close the roof, which was hinged in the middle.

"Goodness, it must be years and years since I last saw that Ark," said Mrs Nelson. "It used to be David's favourite toy, he would never be parted from it. His girls always preferred playing with the doll's house." Jonathan had put the Ark down on the carpet and undone the catch. Lying inside were some little wooden figures which he lifted out and stood up.

"Oh, look!" said Mrs Nelson, "It's Mrs Noah – and the boys – and old Noah himself! It's quite like seeing old friends. To think I could have forgotten Mrs Noah in her apron."

She reached down and stood Mr Noah and Mrs Noah together, and the two little wooden figures of their sons next to them.

"Yes, there should be three sons, of course," she said. "Shem, Ham, and Japhet. Japhet doesn't seem to be here – he was probably lost a long time ago."

Jonathan picked up Mr Noah. He had a nice, calm, carved face and a beard that once had been painted white.

"Well, come along, Jonathan," said his grandmother. "We shall have to be going. Say goodbye to Mrs Nelson."

Jonathan didn't want to go a bit. He wanted to run back up all the stairs to the attic where the toys were to find Mr and Mrs Noah's other son. He was probably in the toy-box, right at the bottom or in that tin. Then he would play at sailing the Ark over the attic floor for a long time and perhaps ride the horse again and … But he had promised his mother to be especially good and polite and to do what his grandmother said without arguing. He sighed softly and put Mr Noah down on the table.

"Goodbye, Mrs Nelson," he said. "Thank you for having me. Can I come again tomorrow morning?"

Jonathan's grandmother seemed to think that this would be rather soon but Mrs Nelson said she would be very pleased to see him.

"I know you have an awful lot to straighten out in the house, my dear," she said, "and Jonathan really will be most welcome to come and play whenever he likes. He won't be in anybody's way and I shall be very glad of his company – and so will the toys." She turned to Jonathan. "Would you like to take the Ark home with you tonight, Jonathan?" she asked, and before the delighted Jonathan had found his voice, she had put the Noah family back into the Ark, fastened the lid, and put it into Jonathan's arms.

Jonathan beamed at Mrs Nelson.

"Oh, thank you," he said. "I'll come tomorrow as early as I can."

The Ark was heavy but Jonathan carried it all the way home by himself, hugging it to him. He did not know quite why but it seemed the best toy he had ever seen, and he could already think of lots of good games to play with it. He stood it on the floor by his chair while he had his tea and his grandfather was very interested to hear all about the rocking horse and other toys.

"Didn't Mrs Nelson say there was a doll's house?" asked his grandmother.

"Oh yes, a great big one," said Jonathan. "I didn't really look at it but I expect Catherine would like it."

He wanted to have the Ark in his bath but his grandmother was unexpectedly firm, saying it looked rather too grimy to go in nice clean bathwater. She stood the Ark on the bathroom stool and had quite a job to get all the dirt from the attic floor off Jonathan's knees. When Jonathan was quite clean and changed into his pyjamas, she tucked him into bed. The Ark was on the wide ledge of the window-seat where he would see it as soon as he woke up, and he had the Noah family to play with in bed. When his grandmother looked in a little while later, Jonathan was fast asleep with Mrs Noah still clasped in one hand.

2

The next morning Jonathan came down to breakfast and found his grandfather in the kitchen.

"Hello, did you sleep well?" asked his grandfather.

"Yes, thank you, Grandpa," said Jonathan. "I had a lovely dream but I can't quite remember what it was about. I know it was a good one, though."

"The best sort of dream," said his grandfather, smiling.

Jonathan put the Ark carefully down on a chair and went across to see what his grandfather was doing. He was slicing tomatoes and mushrooms into a large frying pan and he now put in a lump of butter, sprinkled salt over the pan and put it on the stove. A most delicious smell started to fill the kitchen, and Jonathan helped to lay the table for breakfast. Everything was nicely arranged with Jonathan's favourite large jam-spoon in the marmalade and his grandfather making tea, when his grandmother came into the kitchen.

"Good morning, dear. Good morning, Jonathan," she said, giving them each a kiss in turn. "How lovely of you to get breakfast ready – it does smell good."

They all sat down round the table and ate a very cheerful breakfast. The sun was shining brightly outside and Jonathan was pleased to think that he didn't have to go to school. When he had nearly finished his second piece of toast and marmalade, he said suddenly, "What were their names, Granny? Mr Noah's boys, I mean."

His grandmother looked at his grandfather, who stirred his tea and said, "Shem, Ham, and Japhet."

"Japhet! Yes, that's it," said Jonathan. "He's the one that's missing. And what does 'going calling at Number Seven' mean, Granny?"

"Calling at Number Seven? I've no idea at all, Jonathan," replied his grandmother. "Who said it?"

"Mrs Nelson did. At least, I think so," said Jonathan. "I thought she said it to you."

"Not that I can remember. You must have dreamt it, dear."

"Oh. Well, anyway, can I go straight to find Japhet after breakfast, please?"

"Well, if you could wait for a little while," said his grandfather, "I want to go along to the vicarage myself to talk to the odd-job man. He'll be working there today in the garden and I want him to come and fix the hole in the fence for me. But first of all, I must finish clearing that patch of grass in the front before the sun gets round there and makes it too hot. It won't take me very long and then we can go together."

Jonathan helped his grandmother to clear away the breakfast things and wiped the knives and forks for her while she washed up.

"That was very helpful of you, Jonathan," she said. "I should leave the rest now and run along outside but don't stand too close to Grandpa while he's using the scythe."

Jonathan picked up his Ark and went out to sit on the front doorstep, to watch his grandfather cutting the long grass and nettles under the sitting room windows. The sun was already bright and warm, though dewdrops still clung to the grass in the shade. It was a good place to sit, so Jonathan settled his back against the door frame and began to sail the Ark gently along, with Mr Noah standing at the back to steer and his two big sons looking out for land ahead. Mrs Noah was in the roofed cabin making the beds and deciding what to have for lunch.

"Do you think it would float, Grandpa?" he asked, as his grandfather straightened up and looked at the patch of grass still waiting to be cut.

"What?" asked his grandfather. "Oh, hmm, I don't know. It looks a bit heavy to me but it really depends on the balance of it. I'll tell you what, why don't you go and try it in the rain-barrel while I finish off this job? It won't take me long now."

The rain-barrel! What a good idea. Jonathan was surprised he hadn't thought of it himself. He stood up and picked up the Ark, carefully putting Mr Noah and his sons inside. Then he stopped and said, "But Grandpa ... "

His grandfather was just stooping to start work again with the scythe but he sighed and straightened his back again.

"Well, Jonathan, what's the trouble?"

"Supposing it doesn't float," said Jonathan anxiously. "What if it turns over and sinks? Right down to the bottom."

"Oh, yes, I see. Well, if it does sink, I'll get it out for you when I've finished here," said his grandfather kindly. "We're sure to be able to fish it up again but don't try by yourself, whatever you do. I don't want my grandson drowned in a rain-barrel, so just be careful."

Jonathan laughed. Of course he wouldn't drown himself but it was a long way to the bottom of the barrel, much too far for him to reach and he didn't want to lose his Ark. Well, Mrs Nelson's Ark, really, or David's. She had said it belonged to somebody called David. How lucky that she thought it was all right to lend it to him. Perhaps if he was very careful with it, she would let him keep it for a day or two, or even a week. But anyway, he would go to the vicarage to play with it every single day.

The rain-barrel was newly painted and stood gleaming in the sunlight near the back door, full to the brim with water. Jonathan thought for a bit and then lifted Mr and Mrs Noah and their two sons out and stood them on the concrete path. He didn't want to lose any of them, and although his grandfather would get the Ark out for him if it sank, he might not want to grope about in deep water for the Noah family if it didn't float. The water glinted and shone on the surface but it looked very dark and cold lower down. Jonathan picked up the Ark in both hands and lowered it carefully into the water. Without letting go altogether, he loosened his hold and found that the Ark was floating quite well. The barrel was about twice the length of the Ark at its widest point, so he gave the Ark a little push. It rocked wildly once, then shot across the barrel, hit the side with a bump and rushed straight back again to Jonathan's side, almost squashing his fingers. Surprised and pleased, he laughed to himself, then made waves in the water with his hands. The water was very cold and made him shiver.

The Ark rocked and danced on the little dancing waves, and Jonathan thought of it setting out across the sea in the pouring rain. First it would have sailed down the streets of the town where the Noah family lived, with square white houses on each side nearly covered by the water, and palm trees sticking out here and there, while the rain went on pouring down all around them, and splashing into the sea. Then they would be in deep water, with the wind driving them along and the tops of the hills making little islands. Mr Noah's boys would be making sure that all the animals had straw to lie on and water to drink and that the smaller ones were found safe corners, where they were in no danger of being trampled on by the large animals moving clumsily about the hold. Mr Noah would be looking out for the rocky islands in their way and Mrs Noah would be cooking and cleaning and … Jonathan looked down at the little figures on the path and saw that Mr Noah had fallen over. He picked him up and dusted him carefully with his shirt, which happened to have come untucked, and then held him while he went on watching the Ark. Then, one morning, everybody would wake up and find the sea calm and flat like the water in the barrel, and the sun shining, and the sky blue, and nothing in any direction but water, stretching away to the edge of the world. Jonathan sighed.

"Oh, I wish I could be there," he said to himself.

At that moment his grandfather came round the corner of the house, carrying his scythe.

"Not drowned, I'm pleased to see," he said. "You were so quiet, I was beginning to wonder. Does your Ark float?"

"Yes, oh, yes, look, it floats jolly well," said Jonathan. "I'm sure it could float right across a real pond. Oh, look out, Grandpa, mind!"

He was just in time to save the rest of the Noah family from being trodden on.

"Well, I've finished round there in the front," said his grandfather. "I'm just going to put this scythe away and have a wash, and then I shall be ready to go with you to the vicarage."

He came back from the garage towards the house just as Jonathan was lifting the Ark out of the water and hastily took it from him.

"You were going to soak yourself all down the front, Jonathan," he said. "Look, the whole thing is absolutely dripping. You'd better leave it in the sunshine to dry out before you play with it anymore or you'll get yourself awfully wet. Now let's go in and tidy ourselves up a bit."

Jonathan put the Noah family into the pockets of his shorts and followed his grandfather into the house. His grandmother was on her knees in the hall, sorting bundles of letters and writing paper out of a large box and tidying them into piles. Some things she was putting into the open drawer of a desk. She sent Jonathan upstairs to brush his hair and tuck his shirt in, then he and his grandfather walked along the road to the vicarage.

The Nelsons were having a mid-morning cup of tea and Jonathan and his grandfather were invited to join them in the large kitchen, which was full of sunshine and smelled wonderfully of the hot biscuits Mrs Nelson had just taken out of the oven. She was passing a glass of milk and three warm crumbly biscuits to Jonathan when there was a tap at the back door and a thin brown man in green trousers came rather shyly into the kitchen.

"Ah, Lukey, come in and sit down," said the Vicar, and as the grown-ups drank their tea, they discussed the fence that was to be mended. Lukey talked very little except to say "Ah", or "Might be", but he had bright eyes, like a bird's, which moved from face to face. Jonathan was sitting on the floor in a patch of sunshine, stroking the white cat that had come to sit beside him.

Grandpa was accepting a second cup of tea, so Jonathan asked if he might go up to the attic.

"All right, Jonathan, but don't ride the horse until Lukey has seen it," said Mrs Nelson. "We want to make sure it's quite safe for you. When Lukey finishes his tea, I want him to have a look at it for me and perhaps oil the squeaks. You can find your way up on your own, can't you?"

Jonathan could. He found the right door on the landing, climbed the steep stairs and went straight to the toy-box. The train and his bridge of wooden blocks were just as he had left them, with the other toys piled on the floor beside the box. He leaned over and poked about, lifting more toys out. There was a cricket bat and some stumps, all fallen different ways inside the box, and rather difficult to pull loose, a skipping rope and one or two other toys but no little wooden figure. Jonathan climbed right inside the box to make sure and stood up again to think. Perhaps in that biscuit tin. He climbed out and picked the tin up but the lid was still too hard for him to get off, so Jonathan carried it all the way downstairs to the kitchen again to his grandfather. His grandfather took the lid off for him but the tin held nothing but some toy cars that looked very old, and a few glass marbles, though Jonathan sat on the floor and looked carefully.

"I simply can't find Japhet," he said to Mrs Nelson. "I couldn't bring the Ark back, because it was too wet from sailing in the rain-barrel."

"Oh, never mind that, my dear," said Mrs Nelson. "You don't have to keep all the toys here, you know. You can keep the Ark at your granny's house to play with, if you like, as long as you are staying with her. What is it you can't find? Japhet? Oh, yes, I see. You know, Jonathan, I'm not at all sure you *will* find him after all this time. He may have been lost, or broken and thrown away, years and years ago."

Jonathan played with a car while the grown-ups went on talking. Then he remembered something.

"Mrs Nelson," he said, pulling gently at her sleeve, "what does it mean, going calling at Number Seven?"

Mrs Nelson turned to him, with half an ear still on what her husband was saying.

"What's that, my dear? Number Seven? Oh, that's what the children say when they're playing with the doll's house, you know. But good gracious me," she said, looking properly at Jonathan, "whoever can you have heard saying that? Who said it to you, Jonathan?"

"Well, I *thought* you were talking about Number Seven to my granny, yesterday," said Jonathan. "But she says I must have dreamt it."

"I don't remember saying it," said Mrs Nelson doubtfully. "I haven't even thought about it for a long time. How extraordinary! Well, come on, Lukey, we could go and look at the rocking horse now, if you've got a minute."

"Ah," said Lukey, and scraped his chair back.

"I thought the staircase was a secret," said Jonathan, rather shocked.

"So it is," said Mrs Nelson. "But it's all right for Lukey to know. He doesn't give secrets away."

Jonathan went faster on the stairs than either Lukey or Mrs Nelson, and by the time they reached the door to the attic, he was running back to meet them, smiling his widest smile, and clutching something in his hand.

"Look, look, I've found him, it's Japhet," he said joyfully. "It's Japhet! You were quite right, Mrs Nelson, he was in the doll's house all the time!"

Mrs Nelson looked at Jonathan, then at Japhet, then back at Jonathan in the greatest amazement, seeming hardly to believe her eyes.

"Good gracious, Jonathan," she said at last. "I really don't understand how ... Well, I'm very glad you have found what you were looking for, my dear, but I really can't think how you knew where to look."

Jonathan spent the rest of the morning until it was time to go home for lunch, kneeling on the attic floor with all the Noah family taken out of his pockets and arranged beside him while he played with the train. Shem and Ham were almost the same size as Mr Noah but Japhet was smaller, with a merry face, and a wide-brimmed hat pushed to the back of his head. Jonathan looked at him from time to time, very pleased that he had managed to find him.

Lukey oiled the creaking joints of the rocking horse with a small oil-can from his pocket but then looked at the stirrups and told Mrs Nelson they were not strong enough to bear a boy's weight.

"No, nor yet a mole's," he said. "That leather's like paper. There's a strap outside in the shed would cut up. And he might do with a lick of paint."

He had to unscrew the horse from its heavy frame to carry it downstairs, and when Jonathan came down into the hall, the horse was standing against the wall, seeming to look at him with its large, watchful eye. Lukey came back for it just as Jonathan was going to join his grandfather at the front door where he was saying goodbye to the Vicar and Mrs Nelson.

"If you're about," said Lukey, "I might be painting round three o'clock or so."

It was the first time he had spoken to Jonathan and he did not wait for an answer but picked up the horse and disappeared in the direction of the back door.

* * * *

By bedtime that evening, Jonathan was almost too tired to walk upstairs. He had had an interesting afternoon talking to Lukey as he painted the rocking horse, and he had even been allowed to help a little bit with the stand. Lukey had started by tying up the horse's mane and tail in pieces of rag, to keep them out of the paint. He cut off the old, worn stirrup-leathers with his penknife, which had three blades and a corkscrew. Then he stood the horse on an upturned box and set to work, whistling between his teeth and standing back now and then with his head on one side to see how the work was going.

When he had finished painting the horse white, he prised the lid off the tin of black paint with a screwdriver and said to Jonathan, "Give it a bit of a stir." Jonathan stirred happily away with a stick and then Lukey painted the hooves shiny black. By now the horse has stopped looking old and tired and was beginning to look young and fresh and full of life. Its coat and hooves gleamed and Lukey gave it bright red, flaring nostrils.

In between times, he and Jonathan went to feed the bonfire of garden rubbish which was burning at the far end of the garden. This was almost as much fun as painting and gave each new colour a chance to dry a little bit. At last, when the stand was painted, Lukey took a small brush and very carefully painted the horse's dark, shining eyes, and then the horse really seemed to come alive and ready to go prancing off on his own.

"You *are* a good painter, Lukey," said Jonathan, admiringly.

"Ah," said Lukey. "Had a job once, painting roundabout horses for a fair. Best leave the rags on till the paint dries, and we'll do the stirrups tomorrow." He cleaned his brush on a piece of spare rag, then looked at Jonathan. "Paint that Ark of yours, shall I?" he said suddenly, nodding to where it stood on the ground beside him.

Jonathan turned pink. "Oh, *would* you?" he said. "Do you think we can? It isn't really mine, you know, it's David's. I've only borrowed it."

"Ah, well, no matter what, it'll be all the better for a lick of paint," said Lukey, and picked up the Ark in his thin brown fingers. He painted it green, with a brown deck and a red roof, very neat and tidy. Then he carefully took the Noah family, one at a time and painted them too. Mr Noah's beard was as white as snow, and so was Mrs Noah's apron. Shem was dressed in green, and Ham in brown, but Japhet had a pair of blue trousers and a red shirt and Jonathan thought he looked more pleased with life even than before.

"You can't go touching 'em till tomorrow, now," said Lukey. "They'll all look after theirselves and be best standin' here to get dry, and here's where you'll find them in the morning."

Jonathan had gone with him to have a last look at the bonfire and had come home. He told his grandmother all about what he and Lukey had been busy doing, while he had his tea.

"I'm pleased you've had such a lovely time, darling," she said, "but if you've finished your milk, you must come to bed now. You look simply worn out and those measles haven't been gone very long."

She tucked Jonathan snugly into bed and he was asleep almost before she had turned out the light.

3

H e could hear a voice saying his name. "Jonathan! Wake up, Jonathan! Come on, get your boots on – we're going fishing!" Jonathan sat up in bed, blinking and rubbing his eyes. It was not morning but his bedroom was quite light from a soft pale light flooding in from the landing. He could see the end of his bed, and the chair, and the curtained window. Then the same voice said again, "Jonathan! Come on, quickly, or we'll miss the tide," and there was Japhet beside the bed, smiling at Jonathan and shaking him by the shoulder. "Where are your boots? Quick, we've got to hurry."

In the greatest astonishment, Jonathan stumbled out of bed and across to the cupboard where his Wellington boots were standing and put them on his bare feet. He turned in time to see Japhet jump up on the window-seat and open the curtains a little.

"That's for when you come home," said Japhet. "Come on, we must run."

Jonathan was not at all sure whether he was awake or asleep but he was not going to be left behind and he hurried out of his bedroom door hard on Japhet's heels. The moonlight was pouring in through the window on the stairs to make a pool of light on the landing, and there, rocking gently, was the

Ark, riding at anchor, its gangplank lowered and resting on the carpet.

"Come on, you two," said Ham from the top of the gangplank, and Jonathan and Japhet ran up the gangplank and onto the Ark. Japhet helped Ham raise the gangplank, and Shem, busy with the anchor in the bows, called out, "Ready!" and the Ark bobbed for a moment, nosed slowly round and floated steadily up the beams of moonlight through the cool glass of the closed window and out into the night.

"Gosh!" said Jonathan. "Japhet, how on earth did you get here? What's happening? Where are we going?"

"We're going fishing. Honestly, I thought you'd never wake up," said Japhet, "and I didn't want to go without you, none of us did. We came in on the moonlight. That's why we had to hurry before it moved off the window and we were left stranded there on the landing. In a minute we'll go and help get the fishing nets ready."

Jonathan could not honestly feel he understood but it did not seem to matter and if this was only a dream, it was a better one than any he could remember having before. He had never in his life been so happy to find himself anywhere as he was to be on the Ark with Japhet, sailing smoothly off into the night sky. The air was fresh and cool and the deck rocked gently beneath their feet. Side by side, Jonathan and Japhet leaned their arms on the rail and looked over the side.

The Ark was already high in the air. There below them, as though drowned in moonlight, lay tiny houses and farms, woods and hills and villages, the church steeples shining silver and the trees stirring gently, like seaweed in a current. Jonathan thought for a moment he saw a fish gliding across a meadow until the faint call of an owl drifted up to them and an old ruined castle on a hill-top looked like the wreck of a ship, half buried in the sand. He sighed happily and Japhet turned his head.

"I'm glad you *did* wake up," said Japhet. "Come on, let's go and help the others with the nets."

Jonathan followed him along the deck to where Shem and Ham were already busy, pulling the folds of long brown fishing-nets out of a locker.

"Come on, you two young ones," said Shem cheerfully. "Stretch this one out along the deck and make sure there are no twists in it, and when I sing out, over it goes."

"How's it going there forward, boys?" called the deep voice of Mr Noah from the stern. "We're just about right to start fishing now, I'd say."

"Ready in two shakes, Father," answered Shem. "All right your end, Ham? Right! Over they go!"

Out went the nets over the side of the Ark, and floated wide. Jonathan went to have another look overboard and found he could see nothing but the moonlight all about them and dark-blue depths below.

"Time for cocoa," said Japhet at his elbow. "Come on, Mother will have it all ready and I'm starving."

He opened a door and they went into the cabin, brightly lit by an oil-lamp which swung gently in time to the rocking of the Ark. Mrs Noah was filling six mugs with hot cocoa from a large jug, and a plate of biscuits stood next to them on the scrubbed, wooden table.

"Come and sit down, boys," she said, "but don't burn your tongues, the cocoa is very hot."

Ham came and sat down next to them on the bench beside the table, and then Shem and Mr Noah came in, in their great sea-boots, and sat the other side.

"Calm as can be," said Mr Noah in his deep voice. "She'll steer herself for a while. Ah, it's a glorious night and I can't think how long it has been since we last went fishing." He gulped contentedly at his cocoa, though it was still far too hot for Jonathan even to take a sip.

"Well, we couldn't be going off without young Japhet," said Mrs Noah. "It's a good thing you got him back from Number Seven, Jonathan, else I don't think we should all be here now."

"What made you go visiting there in the first place beats me," said Ham. "I didn't know you were so interested in their fancy ways of going on."

Japhet looked rather sheepish. "Well, I only wanted to have a look at the cars," he said. "There were two new ones outside the front door that afternoon. Then when it was time to tidy up, somebody put me inside the house. It was *awful*. All they want to do is have tea parties all day long. They kept trying to make me join in and be polite. "Come along, Japhet, you sit here next to Cynthia and pass the sandwiches." It's all right you laughing, Shem! It didn't feel at all funny to me. In the end they left me alone – gave me up as a bad job. But gosh, I'm going to be jolly careful never to be left there again."

"Have they really got carpets and lace curtains in all the bedrooms?" asked Mrs Noah curiously.

"I don't know, Mother," said Japhet. "I never even went upstairs. There's a nice big kitchen but none of them can cook proper food. It's just sandwiches all the time, about two each with the crusts cut off, and cups and cups of watery tea. I just gave up and went to sleep until Jonathan came, and all the time I kept dreaming about going on a sea-voyage and eating plates of hot stew."

"Well," said Mr Noah, "We're going to make up for it now. Here we are with a full crew and the weather set fair and nothing to stop us getting our fill of both sea-voyage *and* hot stew, eh, Mother?"

"I knew the minute I heard you talking, Jonathan," said Mrs Noah, "that the Ark would be afloat again in no time."

She smiled warmly at Jonathan who turned rather pink but smiled back. Ham put down his empty mug with a satisfied sigh and stood up.

"How about pulling in the nets, Father?" he said. "Do you think we'll have a catch by now?"

Mr Noah got to his feet. "Yes, come on, lads," he said. "All hands on deck!"

"I think I'll come too, to watch you get the nets in," said Mrs Noah, straightening her apron. "Then I'll have to finish looking through my store-cupboard."

It seemed cooler outside on deck this time and Jonathan was glad of the warm cocoa making his middle glow comfortably inside. Shem went aft to take the wheel while the rest of them crowded to the side and each got ready to haul in the nets. Jonathan took a quick look overboard but could see nothing but blue depths and the sparkle of moonlight.

"What's *in* the net, though?" he was just beginning to say to Japhet, when, "Heave-ho! In she comes," shouted Mr Noah, and they all grabbed at the net and pulled together. "Again! Now, again!" shouted Mr Noah. "What a catch! Here she comes now. One last heave – all together! Heave!" With one last tremendous pull on the net, their feet braced against the side, Jonathan and Japhet brought their end in, and the net spilled its glittering contents onto the deck. They slipped and shone about their feet – like fish, almost, but not quite like fish, and bending down, Jonathan discovered what they were.

"Stars!" he exclaimed in surprise. "Stars! We've caught heaps of stars!" He picked some up in his hands and let them slide through his fingers to the deck again.

Japhet was laughing. "Yes, you see – I thought you'd be surprised. When we go fishing, sometimes we catch fish and sometimes we catch stars. Sometimes fish-fish and sometimes star-fish."

Jonathan burst out laughing too, and the two of them ran along the deck, slipping and sliding in stars, and round to the other side where Mr Noah and Ham were already beginning to haul in the other net.

"It's another huge catch," panted Ham happily. "Come and lend a hand, you two, before it slips back."

Jonathan grasped at the net with both hands and tugged hard, next to Mr Noah. Japhet was beside him still gurgling with laughter, and Mrs Noah came to help Ham. In came the net again and out tumbled the glittering stars in a shining stream on to the deck.

"Oh, I do love to see that pretty sight!" said Mrs Noah. "I never shall get used to it. You've got a fine catch there, my dear, and the night not half over."

Mr Noah and Ham threw the net out again, then Mr Noah stooped to look at the heap of stars. "They're fairly crowding up to be caught tonight," he said. "The big ones will have to go back, of course – we'll get to sorting them in a while. Ham, roll me a couple of empty barrels along here, will you? And you two boys, start sorting out the big ones to throw back."

Jonathan picked up a star in his hand and turned it over, looking at it. It felt cool to his fingers but it throbbed and glowed with its own light.

"Look, Jonathan," said Japhet, who had been sorting stars into heaps, according to size. He picked out a big star and carried it over to the rail. Then he took it by one of its five points, drew his hand back and let go. The star shot over the side in a long, low curve and finally disappeared into the blue.

"Hey, now me!" said Jonathan, scrambling forward with his star. His first throw was not very good. The star flew high in the air and dropped like a stone, only a few feet from the Ark. There was a splash and a little shower of sparkling yellow moonlight fell back on to the surface.

"No, look," said Japhet. "You don't really throw it, it's more of a flick, really. You hold one point – like this – and you bend your wrist back – and zoom!"

The star whizzed overboard, gleaming and twinkling, and from far away they heard a faint splash. Jonathan tried again several times and at last he got the knack of it. It was an amazing feeling when his star flew off, long and low, for the first time and disappeared from view, almost too far away for the splash to be heard.

"Good, good, well done!" shouted Japhet, dancing about. "That's the idea, that was a smashing shot. Let's see you do it again."

Now Ham came and joined in Japhet and Jonathan's game. Not only could he throw further than either of them but if he found a star of the right size and weight he could make it skim along the tops of the waves, bouncing once or twice into the air before it sank at last.

"I'd better go and take a turn at the wheel," he said finally. "Shem'll be wanting to stretch his legs."

They hauled in the nets once or twice more but the catches were not as big as the first enormous ones they had taken. Ham and his father had been scooping heaps of the little stars into the barrels, and Japhet showed Jonathan how to help Shem and Mr Noah fill the barrels with the smallest ones, leaving the big stars on the deck. Then the barrels were trundled along to a hatch and from there they were rolled down a ramp to be stored in the enormous hold of the Ark. It was so big that Jonathan could quite imagine that two elephants would take up hardly any space at all. There were rows and rows of bulging sacks and casks and barrels, some full and some empty, and a pile of folded sacks in a corner. Shem showed them to Jonathan by the light of the lantern he was carrying.

"These casks are full of water and those with the red lines across the lids are oil – one line for cooking oil and two for oil for the lamps," he said. "There are some little kegs of honey here too. The yellow barrels, like the ones we've been filling, are for stars, and the sacks over there –" he raised the lantern so that its bright light fell on them – "are full of potatoes and sugar and all sorts of other things – flour, cocoa, that kind of thing. Japhet, come out of that sugar sack – I can see you!"

Japhet came back round the sacks laughing, and gave Jonathan two lumps of sugar, keeping two more for himself. They went up on deck, each with a bulge in one cheek.

"What do you use the stars for?" Jonathan asked when he had finished his first lump.

"Oh, they make good ballast and they come in handy for all sorts of things," said Japhet, vaguely. "You'll see."

"But why only little ones?" said Jonathan. "Why do you throw the big ones back?"

Japhet looked surprised. "Well, you know, all the stars big enough to see from down there," he waved his hand down in the direction of the earth, "have proper names and everything, and they are useful where they are. Sailors steer by them and have proper star-charts and things, and men look at them through big telescopes and write books about them. They would be missed if they weren't there any more and my father says it would cause an awful bother. When you throw them back, they swim away to their proper places. But the little ones we keep, and there are millions of those – they never seem to get any fewer, however many we catch."

"Anyway," said Jonathan, "it's the best sort of fishing I ever heard of."

By now all the big stars had been sent spinning overboard, the nets shaken and folded and put away in their lockers, and the decks swept clear of stardust.

"About time we put back, I'm thinking," said Mr Noah, "if we don't want to miss the tide. Japhet, ask your mother if she's got another mug of that cocoa and bring it to me in the wheelhouse. I'll take over from Ham now for the trip back."

Jonathan and Japhet reached the cabin door at the same time as Shem, who was coming from the other direction.

"Mother," said Shem, "is there something to eat? I'm famished."

"I never knew any of you when you *weren't* famished," said Mrs Noah, smiling. She turned round from her store cupboard, a list in one hand and a pencil in the other. "And four bags of flour. There! Now, sit yourself down at the table, Shem, and I'll find you something to eat. Are you boys going to take this cocoa along for me?" She poured out a mug of cocoa for Shem and gave Japhet the jug to carry to his father. Jonathan had two mugs in one hand and a little dish-shaped basket full of sandwiches in the other. They carried them carefully along the deck to where Mr Noah was at the wheel talking to Ham, who was bending over a chart and following a dotted line with his finger. The Ark was moving faster now and their wake stretched behind them in a straight, shining line towards the bright face of the moon.

Jonathan and Japhet hurried back along the deck to the cabin and sat side by side on the bench next to the table, eating sandwiches and taking sips of hot, sweet cocoa. Jonathan began to feel sleepy. He leaned his elbows on the blue and white squared tablecloth and his head on his hands.

"Nearly home, Jonathan," said Shem kindly.

"Good gracious me, look at the boy, he's nearly asleep!" exclaimed Mrs Noah. "You'll be glad of your bed, Jonathan, I can see, but don't go to sleep before we get you safely home, now!"

Jonathan smiled a sleepy smile and at that moment Ham came into the cabin, making the oil-lamp leap and flicker in the sudden draught. "Just coming in now," he said cheerfully. "Come on, Jonathan, we shan't have more than a moment to wait before we're away again."

Jonathan stumbled out on deck with Japhet yawning beside him, and saw that once more houses and trees could be seen below them in the moonlight. He blinked and rubbed his eyes to keep awake as he leaned against the rail. As if in a dream he saw the railway line gleaming down there and curving away into the distance, fields coming up closer beneath the Ark, a road, a wood, quite close now. A white horse came out of the wood as he watched and stood a moment, its head proudly up, seeming to smell the wind. Then it was off at a gallop, down a hill, across the meadow below them and out of sight, its white mane flying, its tail streaming behind as it disappeared beneath the side of the Ark.

Jonathan lifted his head, and there, close ahead of them, was his grandfather's house, the moonlight shining full on the bedroom windows. The Ark floated steadily down the moonlight until they could see its shadow on Jonathan's window, growing larger and larger. Jonathan gasped with the sudden chill as they came through the glass of the window, and then the Ark was bobbing quietly on the window-seat in a pool of moonlight which came through the gap Japhet had made in the curtains. Shem and Ham lowered the gangplank and Japhet came to the bottom with Jonathan, who by now was almost entirely asleep.

"Goodnight," said Japhet. "Don't forget to take off your boots. Don't go to bed in your boots, Jonathan!"

Jonathan sat yawning and blinking on the window-seat and pulled off his boots, while already beside him the Ark was putting about and rising towards the window. He let the boots drop to the floor, climbed into bed, shivering a little, and fell fast asleep.

4

The sun was shining brightly next morning when Jonathan came down to breakfast and the day seemed to stretch in front of him, warm and sunny and ready to be filled with anything he felt like doing. His grandmother asked if he would like to walk down to the village with her to do some shopping but Jonathan had remembered that Lukey was coming to mend the fence and said he would rather watch.

"Ah, yes, much more interesting for you," said grandmother. "As long as you don't stand too close and get in his way. I shan't be gone very long."

When Lukey arrived, he was carrying a long thin plank of wood over his shoulder and both its ends danced up and down in the sunshine in time to his footsteps. Grandpa showed him the place where the fence was leaning right out over the meadow behind the house, and Lukey hung his jacket on a post and set to work straight away to take out the broken planks. He whistled tunefully as he worked, making as much noise as three or four people whistling at once, Jonathan thought.

"How old were you when you learned to whistle?" he asked when Lukey paused for a moment with his head on one side to look at the fence. Lukey laughed, showing his white teeth.

"Me? I was born whistling, pretty near," he said, "same as a thrush might be." He wrenched another piece of rotten wood out and laid it beside the others on the grass. "All it wants is practice. Try a lick with your tongue to get you started off."

Jonathan had a good lick at the corners of his mouth and tried again as he followed Lukey as he went to get his grandfather's saw. Lukey measured along his plank of wood and made some marks with a small stump of pencil taken from his pocket. The he sawed the plank into pieces using an upturned box to rest on. Jonathan gazed at the little hills of sawdust, growing as if by magic in the grass beneath the cutting saw.

"I thought I saw the rocking horse last night," he said suddenly, without thinking. "Only, its mane wasn't tied up." Then he remembered it had only been a dream and opened his mouth to say so.

"Ah," said Lukey calmly, carrying the first sawn-off piece of wood over to the fence. "Took them rags off last night, once the paint wasn't too tacky. Didn't want him in curling rags too long."

Jonathan's heart surprised him by giving a great thump. Perhaps, after all, it had not been a dream? But in that case, the Ark, the fishing, Japhet … He realised his mouth was still open and closed it, then without thinking he licked his lips and blew. Lukey raised his head, grinning widely.

"There you are!" he said admiringly. "Whistling. Be whistling yourself half to death by the end of the week, I shouldn't wonder."

By lunchtime the fence was finished and the staring white of the new planks stained with creosote to match the rest.

Lukey had let Jonathan do one whole plank. The creosote looked like coffee without milk and smelt of tar. Jonathan had whistled the whole time, all on one note, and Lukey had said he would soon be whistling any tune he put his mind to.

His grandfather was pleased with the fence and to hear that Jonathan had learnt to whistle (though he said he would rather he did not do so at the table) and his grandmother was even more glad to see that Jonathan had got his appetite back after his measles. After lunch, Jonathan set off towards the vicarage, whistling as he went, to find Japhet.

He was not quite sure what he had expected to find but he was certainly surprised, and rather disappointed, to find the rocking horse, the Ark and the Noah family exactly as Lukey had left them the evening before, standing in the doorway of the shed. Japhet stood in his place between Mr Noah and Shem, a very small, painted, wooden figure. Jonathan picked him up in his hand to look at him.

"Oh, Jonathan," said Mrs Nelson's voice, and Jonathan looked up to see her coming towards him, carrying a large pair of shoes in one hand and a pair of kitchen scissors in the other. "Hello, my dear, how nice to see you. I wonder if you would be very kind and take these shoes up to the attic for me? Somebody has given them to me for the next jumble sale, just as I was on my way to cut some sweet peas."

Jonathan held out his hand and took the shoes but they were large, men's shoes, heavy enough to need two hands. He put them down on the ground for a moment, arranged Japhet carefully in one shoe, and picked them up to carry them upstairs to the attic. The sunshine was streaming in through the window in the ceiling at the top of the secret stairs and was making a yellow patch quite high on the wall. There was an empty-looking space where the rocking horse had been standing but the other toys were spread over the floor as he had left them.

It was lovely, thought Jonathan, not to have to tidy away the toys each day. It so often seemed to happen at home that he had just finished arranging a racing-track for his cars, or a farm, or a fight between two tribes of Indians, on his bedroom floor, and then was asked to clear up before tea, when he had not even really started the actual game at all. But here in the attic, nobody minded a bit if he left all the toys set out, ready to play with whenever he liked. Perhaps Lukey would put new stirrups on the horse soon and bring it back up to its place in the attic and he would go for a long gallop.

Jonathan realised he was still holding the shoes and wondered where he should put them. He looked down at them, brown and shiny, with Japhet propped up in one of them, and smiled.

"Hey, Japhet," he said, putting both shoes on the floor and kneeling beside them. "You look as though you're driving that shoe."

"Driving a shoe?" said Japhet, looking surprised and not at all wooden, as soon as Jonathan spoke to him. "I thought you meant it for a boat."

"Well, I suppose it could be a boat," said Jonathan, "but the shop where my father gets shoes mended has a picture outside, over the door, of a racing-driver sitting in a shoe and driving like mad. I always like looking at it and thinking about it. Just imagine what fun it would be, driving a shoe."

"It sounds smashing," said Japhet, climbing out of the shoe and looking at it. "Is the shoe just the same as this?"

Jonathan thought for a moment. "Not exactly the same," he said. "It's brown, all right, but it hasn't got laces. There is a steering wheel in it, and the driver has a special hat on in case he crashes – that's it, a crash helmet."

Japhet walked halfway round his shoe and back again. Then he looked at Jonathan. "We haven't got a steering wheel but we *have* got laces," he said. "I bet you could steer with those. Come on, let's try."

"All right," said Jonathan joyfully. "I'll take this one and we'll have a race."

They each leapt into a shoe and seized the ends of the laces, one in each hand. Nothing at all happened. Japhet looked at Jonathan and Jonathan looked back at Japhet.

"You take the brake off," said Japhet (they each put out a hand and took off an imaginary brake), "turn on the engine –"

"– and you put your foot down," said Jonathan and jammed his foot down on an imaginary accelerator.

At once his shoe was off with a jerk and rushed across the attic floor, closely followed by Japhet's. Jonathan was rather taken by surprise and swerved from side to side as he shot straight towards the train but he managed to get control of his shoe just in time to round the corner of the toy-box with a sharp pull on his left shoe-lace, narrowly missing the wooden engine. He stopped feeling alarmed, and as he began to enjoy himself he started to make the right sort of engine noises in his throat – a load roar for the engine, a squeal of tyres as he slowed down sharply for a turn in the far corner of the attic, and the noise of clashing gears as he accelerated off again between the table-legs. Japhet, who had been watching his chance, cut off a corner and caught him up and they were speeding along together, side by side, crouched in their shoes and making a deafening noise of racing engines.

They zoomed past the doll's house and two dolls who had opened the front door to go for a walk stepped hastily back inside and closed it again. They went flying three times side by side over the level crossing, in front of the train, before the gate-keeper managed to close the gates and wave the engine-driver on, and a man changing a tyre on one of the little cars that had been in the biscuit-tin straightened up and shaded his eyes with his hand as they went howling past him and shot out of sight in a cloud of dust. They tore along between a chair and the wall, and Jonathan wondered what had become of Japhet's hat, then nearly ran over it as it lay in his path.

Japhet had got ahead now and was swerving from side to side so that Jonathan could not come up beside him, laughing uproariously and leaning first one way and then the other as his shoe rocked about. Jonathan kept close behind him, waiting for a chance to overtake, and as they came thundering under the table and out the other side, he put his foot down as hard as he could. His shoe seemed to leap forward and he was up beside the startled Japhet, neck and neck, almost passing him. Then Japhet gave one last swerve, the two shoes crashed into each other at top speed and suddenly Jonathan was flying through the air to land with a thump on the rolled-up carpet by the wall, with Japhet sprawling on his face next to him. The two shoes had fallen over but did not seem to have come to any harm and, rather to his surprise, Jonathan found that he was not hurt either.

"Are you all right, Japhet?" he said anxiously.

Japhet lifted his head. He was scarlet in the face and still gasping for breath but he managed to laugh. "I think so," he said, and sat up. "I must say, Jonathan, you think of good things to do. I would never have thought of driving a shoe like a racing-car."

"Oh, I've thought about it often," said Jonathan, sliding down the carpet and helping to turn the shoes the right way up, "but I would never really have done it without you, and this attic is just the place for it. This can be the racing garage," he said, putting the shoes under a chair. "Let's race again tomorrow."

"All right," said Japhet, brushing some dust off his hat. "That was super. I bet Ham will want a go when we tell him about it."

"What shall we do next?" asked Jonathan. "It's just the right sort of afternoon for a sail, really."

"Oh, yes, Father wondered if you'd like to come on the river," said Japhet. "He thought we might go down nearly as far as the mill and stop at the island."

"The island? Gosh!" said Jonathan. "I'll go and get the Ark now." He went quickly downstairs and outside to find the Ark, leaving Japhet playing marbles in the attic. He had put Mr and Mrs Noah, Shem, and Ham carefully into the Ark and was turning to go, when Lukey came past, carrying a ladder.

"Hello, Lukey," said Jonathan. "Look how nicely the paint has dried."

"Ah. Be cutting up straps for stirrups later," said Lukey. "You'll maybe get a ride if you're still about."

"What time?" asked Jonathan. "I have to be home by half-past five at the latest, I promised my granny."

"Oh, it'll be before then. Soon after six is when the rabbits starts and I like to take a stroll along."

"The rabbits start what?" asked Jonathan.

"Oh, their playin' and their dancin'," said Lukey, casually. "Real pretty it can be, to watch them at it." He shouldered his ladder again and walked on, and Jonathan hurried back upstairs to the attic.

5

How strange that the Ark was no more than a toy as Jonathan carried it along and yet, once he had set it down and Japhet had scrambled up from his game of marbles, it was a real Ark, floating on the attic floor. Jonathan and Japhet hurried up the gangplank and watched Ham pull the dripping anchor aboard before going along to the stern to talk to Mr Noah in the wheelhouse. Shem was steering, while Mr Noah was folding a large chart to put it away. He took another chart from a locker and spread it flat on the table.

"Here we are," he said. "Look here, you two boys. This is where we are going – down the stream at the bottom of the vicarage garden, along the river and almost to the mill. We'll stop here at the island, for a picnic. This is where we are now, just where the stream runs along behind the church."

Jonathan and Japhet looked at the brown finger of Mr Noah on the chart, then went outside on deck and found that, sure enough, they were already out in the open air and sailing down the stream. There was the square tower of the church, visible above the trees on the nearer bank. The Ark was moving along at a steady pace and the water was rippling and gurgling along its sides. The afternoon was warm and sunny, and the two boys leaned contentedly on the rail, watching the banks slip by and keeping their eyes open for water-rats or otters.

About a mile and a half downstream, Mr Noah took the tiller and carefully navigated a narrow, winding channel through a thick bed of weeds which opened into the river itself. Now the Ark was gliding quickly along between flat meadows where cows were grazing or wading into the shallows to drink. Two swans with a family of cygnets drifted by and Mrs Noah threw some stale bread overboard to them. The sunlight danced on the water, and now and then Jonathan heard the splash of a fish jumping. Twice they sailed under bridges where the road crossed the river, and one of the bridges was like a little green tunnel with big yellow kingcups growing at each end.

"This is a super place for a hideout," said Jonathan.

"We could be smugglers," said Japhet, "or river pirates."

A lorry with a load of empty milk churns clattered and banged over the bridge above their heads, making them laugh and put their fingers in their ears until it had gone. Once they were past the second bridge, Mr Noah kept the Ark close to the left bank of the river and Jonathan and Japhet amused themselves by picking leaves from the overhanging branches as they passed underneath.

"We're keeping well over, out of the current that goes down over the waterfall," said Shem. "Look, you can see now where the river divides."

Sure enough, when they looked, the boys could see that they were following the slow, quiet branch of the river which was the mill-stream, while over to their right the water tumbled and leaped over the waterfall carrying loose sticks and leaves with it at a speed that showed how fast the current was running. They were not long in rounding the next bend and there was the island close ahead, small, covered in grass and trees, and with not another boat in sight. Mr Noah brought the Ark carefully alongside the island and Shem and Ham made fast at the bows and the stern to two trees.

"I'm glad to see you're looking after my new paint," said Mr Noah, smiling in his beard.

Mrs Noah spread a red tablecloth on the grass under the trees and Ham carried the large picnic basket down for her. There were egg sandwiches, tomato sandwiches, and cheese sandwiches, a large jam sponge and apples for anybody who was still hungry.

"No ham sandwiches, I see," said Japhet.

"You be careful, young Japhet," said Ham threateningly, "or I'll turn you into Japhet pie and throw you to the fishes."

They lay sprawled on the grass in the shade and ate and talked and laughed and found a corner for just one more sandwich, until they could really eat no more. Then Jonathan and Japhet went off to explore the island. They found two thick holly trees which grew together, making a little house in the middle – if you could get in without getting too scratched by the prickly leaves. They managed to wriggle in when Jonathan discovered a kind of tunnel, where the branches did not reach quite to the ground. When they had crawled out again they went to the water's edge at the far side of the island and saw a bright flash of colour which was kingfisher darting upstream. At the next bend in the river past the island, the water dropped and tumbled over the mill wheel, and the roof of the mill could just be seen above the trees.

"I hope I won't be back too late," said Jonathan.

"It's all right," said Japhet. "You'll never get back too late when you're on the Ark. Father will make sure of it. But perhaps we should go back and find the others now. Let's see how close we can get without them seeing us."

It was fun creeping from tree to tree on their way back across the island, and when they were almost back at the picnic place they lay flat and wriggled forward on their stomachs, like Indians. They were in sight of Mrs Noah, packing things back into her basket and talking to Mr Noah, who was sitting comfortably propped up against a tree, smoking his pipe, when Japhet crawled over a thick bramble. A loud yell would have ruined the game and he managed to stop himself in time, and with an expression of great agony silently removed several thorns from his hand. He made a face at Jonathan, who was laughing at him, and they wriggled forward again.

"Now, where can those two young ones have got to?" said Mrs Noah placidly.

"Oh, the other end of the island and up a tree, I daresay," answered Mr Noah, and Jonathan and Japhet, delighted, leapt up with a shout.

Shem and Ham had been fishing with lines and came back now with four or five fair-sized fish in a basket, and they all set off again up the river in the direction of home. Jonathan talked to Mr Noah in the wheelhouse, as Mr Noah contentedly steered his Ark along the stretch of river near the waterfall.

"How does the Ark go so fast, even against the current?" asked Jonathan. "It doesn't have an engine, or sails."

Mr Noah smiled. "The Ark doesn't always follow the same rules as other craft," he said. "She always goes where she's going, upstream or down, with or against the tide, and she travels at her own speed, fast or slow."

"Do you ever sail through storms?" asked Jonathan after they had passed the roar of the waterfall. Shem, who was nearby, laughed aloud and Mr Noah laughed, too.

"Storms?" he repeated. "Storms, did you say? Lord bless you, Jonathan, the Ark was built for storms and floods. Nothing we like more than a good strong gale blowing, rain coming down its hardest, thunder fit to deafen you and plenty of lightning to give us glimpses of the crashing waves. That's real Ark-weather, that is, when the whole crew needs to keep its wits awake."

"Gosh," said Jonathan, "it does sound exciting. I'd love to be with you in a storm."

After a glance at Jonathan's eager face and shining eyes, Mr Noah sailed on for a few minutes without answering. Finally he said, "I'm thinking we might set out on a long voyage soon. We'll have to see which provisions are running low and so on before deciding where to make for, of course. We might well meet with a storm or two if we go far."

Japhet put his head round the door. "Come on, Jonathan," he said. "We'll soon be up to that bridge again, and we can be smugglers if you come out on deck."

Jonathan went out with Japhet and looked at the sky. There was hardly a cloud to be seen unless you counted one or two very wispy ones very high up. There certainly seemed no chance of a storm that afternoon.

"How long does it take, when you go on a real voyage, Japhet?" he asked.

"Oh, it all depends where we go," said Japhet, leaning over the side of the Ark and looking upstream. "Might be ten days or so, or it could be six weeks or even a year. More if we went right round the world."

"Oh, well, then, that's no good," said Jonathan sadly. "I shan't be able to come."

Japhet almost overbalanced into the river in horror.

"Not *come?*" he exclaimed. "Not come if we go on a voyage?" He kicked wildly with his feet and landed back on the deck to look at Jonathan. "Of course you'll have to come with us, it wouldn't be fun at all without you."

"Yes, but I can't, really," said Jonathan. "You see, I'm only staying with my Granny for a week or so. 'A week or ten days' they said, and I've been there for days and days already."

Japhet gave a great sigh of relief. "Oh, is *that* all," he said. "Goodness, Jonathan, you did give me a shock. That means a week or ten days of *their* time. *Our* time works quite differently. I can't explain it very well but I expect my father will, or my mother, if you ask. Anyway, everything will be all right, you just wait and see, and we'll have great fun. Did my father tell you where we will be going?"

"No, he doesn't seem to have decided yet," said Jonathan, feeling rather unsure still but much happier. "He didn't say anything about going right round the world, anyway. I'm sure I couldn't come for a whole year."

"Yes, but don't you see – oh, look out, Jonathan, here's the bridge," Japhet was just beginning to say, when from a long way away, above the noise of the water, Jonathan seemed to hear his grandmother's voice calling his name.

"Jonathan!"

There it was again, much clearer this time, and all in a moment there was a rush and a blur of the green river-bank, and Jonathan found himself kneeling on the floor of the attic feeling slightly breathless, and with the Ark, small and wooden and gaily painted, on the floor in front of him.

"Yes, all right, Granny," he called back. "I'm just coming."

He ran downstairs and found his grandmother talking to Mrs Nelson in the hall.

"Hello, Jonathan," she said. "The ice cream van came along, and Grandpa has bought some ice cream, so I thought I would come and find you before it melts. Have you been having fun?"

"Oh, yes, great fun, I've been playing with the Ark," said Jonathan. "Lukey's going to mend the horse later on."

He said goodbye to Mrs Nelson and walked home along the lane with his grandmother. His grandfather was in the kitchen, washing his hands under the tap and humming happily.

"It's gone very well today," he said. "One more good drive at it tomorrow and the whole garden should be tidy and ready to be fertilised and planted. The Vicar was telling me he goes to a good nursery for roses and will take me there to look round. Well, come along, let's take some chairs outside, Jonathan, and we can all eat our ice creams."

After the huge picnic they had all eaten on the island, Jonathan had been sure he would need no more at all to eat before breakfast the next day but he found he was surprisingly hungry, and even after he had eaten ice cream in the garden with his grandparents, tea was a welcome sight. In the middle of his tea, Jonathan remembered there was a question he wanted to ask.

"Grandpa," he said, "is it true that rabbits dance?"

"Dance?" repeated his grandfather in surprise. "Rabbits? How do you mean, Jonathan, with music and so on? I've heard of dancing bears, or even elephants but not rabbits, as far as I can remember."

Jonathan looked doubtful. "He didn't say anything about music," he said. "It was Lukey. He said he liked to go for a walk just after six o'clock to see the rabbits dancing and playing."

His grandfather laughed out loud. "Oh, you quite relieve me," he said. "*Wild* rabbits, you mean. Yes, it's quite true that they come out to frolic about in the evenings, and I suppose you could call it dancing when they hop and skip about in the grass. I'll tell you what, Jonathan. If we can persuade your grandmother to let you stay up late one evening before you go home, perhaps we could go for a walk ourselves to see if we can't catch a glimpse of them dancing."

"Oh, Granny! Will you let me?" begged Jonathan.

Granny smiled. "I expect between the two of you, you will manage to persuade me," she said. "I'm glad to say Jonathan looks better every day, and he's being awfully good at amusing himself happily. I should think tomorrow, or the day after, we could try to find some rabbits as long as it doesn't rain."

Jonathan was delighted. "Gosh, how super!" he said, bouncing on his chair. "I'll go to sleep most terribly fast tonight, Granny, so that you really will let me go," and either because he had promised or because his eyes simply would not stay open, he was asleep very soon after climbing into bed.

6

When Jonathan climbed up the stairs to the attic the next morning, wondering happily what he would do today, he found that Lukey had been there before him. There on its stand was the horse, its coat gleaming, its neck arched, and with new stirrup-leathers hanging from the saddle.

"Oh!" said Jonathan, and rushing across the room he gave the horse a hug round the neck. "I *am* glad you're ready for a ride."

He climbed happily into the saddle, picked up the smart new leather reins, smoothed the horse's tangled mane, and off he went. He rocked quite slowly at first, until he felt at home in the saddle and not frightened of falling off. He looked about as he rode and saw the toy cars driving about the attic floor and the engine-driver drinking a mug of tea and chatting with the man who looked after the level crossing. Somebody was busy in the doll's house, too, to judge from the duster being shaken out of an upstairs window. The Ark was on the other side of the toy-box, out of sight.

Jonathan began to go faster, until the toys went into a blur and even the walls of the attic became hazy and indistinct. "Come on, boy," he said joyfully, going faster still, and all at once they were out in the fresh air, cantering fast across a field towards a hedge. Jonathan laughed out loud as he felt the horse gather itself together under him for the jump and clear the hedge like a bird.

Now they were riding through a wood, with a brown carpet of leaves under the horse's hooves and bright green ferns growing beneath the trees. A cloud of pale-yellow butterflies fluttered across their path and out of sight, and they rode on, more slowly now as the path twisted and turned through the trees. Birds were singing gaily, and a large jay flew across screaming an alarm as they came near. The horse slowed to cross a plank bridging a stream, then trotted up a rise to where the path ended at the edge of the wood.

They came out of the trees into the sunlight, and there in front of them was a long, rolling stretch of open country with smooth turf underfoot. Jonathan felt the horse quiver all over with excitement as they stopped for a moment to look and to enjoy the coolness of the breeze on their faces. Then it snorted with joy, tossing its head wildly, and Jonathan gripped tightly with his knees as they set off at a gallop, thundering headlong down the long slope of the hillside. They tore along as if into battle, the pounding hoofbeats muffled by the green grass that smelt sweet and warm in the sunshine. The wind blew Jonathan's hair straight up on end and he felt as if he were flying as they swept across the valley and up the opposite hillside at full gallop, with the horse frisking its tail for the sheer joy of being alive.

"Over the hills and far away," thought Jonathan and he opened his mouth to shout it but the wind snatched the words away over his shoulder as they topped the rise and went galloping on.

It seemed they galloped for miles before the horse began to tire. At last he slowed to a walk until he reached the shade of a large oak tree on a hill, and stopped there for a rest. Jonathan slid to the ground and flung himself flat on his back under the tree to cool off while the horse stood quietly, chewing mouthfuls of sweet grass and swishing the flies away from Jonathan and himself with his long tail.

When they were rested, Jonathan mounted again, expecting the horse to turn back the way they had come but the horse, who appeared to know just where he was going, set off at an easy canter down the further slope of the hill. There were two horses and a foal grazing there, and they raised their heads and whinnied in greeting as Jonathan and the horse came down the hillside.

"Come on, boy, let's race!" said Jonathan, and at once felt the horse gather itself and lengthen its stride.

The black mare and the chestnut horse wheeled round and raced neck and neck with them across the grass. The little foal was left far behind and its mother soon turned back to wait for it, leaving Jonathan's horse and the chestnut racing together up the hill. Suddenly, as Jonathan raised his head to look in front of him, he saw they were almost back to the edge of the wood, and realised that they must have travelled in a wide circle. As they slowed down, the chestnut horse swerved away, tossing its mane, to go back down the hillside to his companions, and Jonathan's horse walked into the shadowy wood and across the plank bridge.

It was just as they had crossed the stream that they met the fox. It stood stock still, looking at them, its eyes very bright and alert and its sharp ears pricked forward. The horse stopped and for a long, long moment Jonathan and the fox stared at one another. At last, the fox suddenly grinned, a wide, mocking grin, letting its tongue loll out of the side of its mouth, and swaggered on across the path to disappear between the clumps of fern.

"Gosh!" said Jonathan, almost too amazed to talk. "A real fox! And he looked right at me! He looked as if he was going to talk. I wonder if he could? I expect he could if he really wanted to."

The rode on through the wood and jumped the hedge back into the field where they had been before. Jonathan noticed the vicarage chimneys sticking up above the trees in front of them as they went very fast across the field. Then the horse steadied himself for such an enormous leap that Jonathan shut his eyes while they flew through the air. The horse landed smoothly and came to a standstill as Jonathan opened his eyes to find himself back in the attic and the horse rocking gently on its stand. He slid off the horse's back and stroked and patted its neck as he said thank you for the ride. Then, as his stomach seemed to be telling him that it was time, he went home for lunch.

His grandfather was rather silent and absent-minded during the meal, as though he were worried, or at least thinking about something tiresome. When his grandmother got up to make a cup of tea as usual, he lowered himself slowly into his big armchair, as if it were a fragile piece of furniture that might break.

"Is something the matter, dear?" asked Granny.

"Oh, just a touch of lumbago, I should think," said Grandpa, carelessly. "Bit of an ache in my back."

Granny put the teapot down and looked at him hard.

"Oh dear, John," she said. "You've done too much heavy work out there in the garden. I shouldn't have let you go at it so hard. You could have got somebody in to help you. Lukey would have come. Where does your back hurt? Here now, let me wedge a cushion in behind you. You'll just have to put your feet up and take things easy this afternoon."

Much to Jonathan's surprise, instead of laughing and saying it was all nonsense, his grandfather actually allowed himself to be settled comfortably with a cushion and a footstool and his newspaper, and even so, went on looking worried and unwell.

Jonathan went back along the lane to the vicarage, where Mrs Nelson let him in to go and play in the attic.

"Do you know where Lukey is, Mrs Nelson?" asked Jonathan. "He has mended the rocking horse, and I wanted to tell him about the ride I had this morning."

"Oh, Lukey isn't about today," said Mrs Nelson. "He does sometimes disappear for a while, you know."

"Disappear?" repeated Jonathan. "Where does he go?"

"I never ask him," said Mrs Nelson. "That's Lukey's own private business. He usually goes for two or three days, sometimes a week. Once he was away for nearly three months, and I was getting quite worried about him. The garden was getting dreadfully overgrown, too. Lukey's got wanderlust in his blood, you know. He likes to feel free to come and go."

Jonathan was most interested to hear this. Now he came to think about it, Lukey did look and seem different from all the other grown-ups he knew, though he could not have explained how. Wanderlust must account for it.

"I hope I see him again before I go home," said Jonathan.

"Well, dear, even if you don't, you'll be coming often to see your granny, won't you?" said Mrs Nelson. "And when you do, you'll always be most welcome to come here to look for Lukey."

Jonathan went upstairs to find Japhet, who had got quite a large bruise from trying to walk on his hands and was now practising climbing a rope instead, rather more successfully. Shem had managed to fix a rope to the top of the toy-box, and Japhet could get about halfway up it by bracing his feet against the side of the box. Once he reached halfway, his arms began to feel tired and he had to slide down to the bottom again.

"Hello, Jonathan," said Japhet. "I was beginning to wonder where you were. Come and have a turn."

The two of them had a very good time climbing the rope, and in between times, Jonathan told Japhet about his ride on the horse and meeting the fox. They were beginning to feel rather tired, when they heard Ham calling from the Ark and hurried up the gangplank into the cabin.

Everybody was sitting round the table and Mr Noah, who had several lists in his hand and a pencil and pad of paper on the table in front of him, was smiling contentedly in his beard. Shem moved up to make room for Jonathan and Japhet to sit together and they looked expectantly at Mr Noah.

"Well, now, let's talk about this voyage," he said in his deep, calm voice. "The stores in the hold have been checked and Mother's counted her provisions in the store cupboard here, and we find there are several things we shall need to stock up with sooner or later. Tea is running low. We could go to India for tea, or China if we preferred. We mostly get our cocoa from Africa and our honey from Greece, and we shall need supplies of both fairly soon. Then we're running pretty short of sugar, and Mother says if we get some oranges while we're about it she'll make a batch of marmalade. What do you all feel about it?"

A babble of excited discussion broke out round the table as the Noah family talked it over, but Jonathan, sitting amongst them, felt too astonished to talk. His own family did not drink much cocoa and in any case they got it from the grocer, not Africa, and they got their tea, and sugar, and honey, yes, and marmalade, too, all from the same place. The idea of sailing to different parts of the world to fill the barrels and sacks in the hold as stocks of different foodstuffs ran low, was a new and exciting one to him. Shem was talking to his father about a trip to China and Ham was saying he thought it was about time they made the voyage to New Zealand again, as calmly as if the world was the size of a duck pond, or at most, a small lake.

"But then, we must have sugar," said Shem, "and there's only a jar or so of mother's marmalade left."

"Where do you get sugar?" asked Jonathan.

"In the West Indies," said Ham. "It's a splendid voyage. There are parrots and pelicans."

"Bananas and coconuts," said Mr Noah.

"And flying fish," added Mrs Noah.

"People play music on the beach – all night, sometimes," said Shem. "You can hear it if you are close enough inshore."

"We found a wreck once," said Japhet, "and went diving."

Jonathan's eyes shone. "Oh!" he said, "I should love to go there more than anywhere in the world. Please could we go to get sugar, Mr Noah?"

"And spices. My spices could do with being added to," put in Mrs Noah, "once we're in those waters."

Mr Noah's eyes travelled from face to face round the table, taking in their expressions. Jonathan held his breath.

"We'll say sugar, then," said Mr Noah. "The West Indies it is, to take on a cargo of sugar, fresh fruit and spices. We can call in for Spanish oranges on the homeward voyage. We'll sail tomorrow."

Everybody cheered, and Ham almost overbalanced as he rocked backwards in his chair. Jonathan was sitting opposite Mrs Noah, and he leaned forward across the table to talk to her.

"Is it *really* all right for me to come?" he said. "Won't my granny be worried if I'm away too long?"

"No, no, it will be all right, Jonathan," Mrs Noah assured him. "It won't seem long to her – just a morning spent playing with the Ark."

"Is that all?" said Jonathan. "I remember before, when we were on the river, she called me … "

"And you heard, and came straight back," said Mrs Noah. "It will be just the same on the voyage. Your granny will never even know you've been away," and she smiled at him kindly.

Jonathan knew that, even if he did not altogether understand, he could take Mrs Noah's word for anything as being absolutely reliable. His last doubts vanished and he joined in the happy discussion going on round the table.

Mrs Noah was not a person to sit down for long, so she began to move about the cabin and put on an apron to do some cooking. Mr Noah and Shem were looking at a chart Shem had fetched from the wheelhouse, and talking about prevailing winds and landfalls and other more mysterious things still. Ham was sitting on a chair, with a leg each side and his elbows resting on the back, playing his mouth-organ, and Jonathan and Japhet were talking about wrecks and islands and pirates, at the same time taking a keen interest in the apple pie Mrs Noah was making and taking little trimmings of pastry when there seemed to be some to spare.

When the pie was in the oven, Japhet went with Ham to the hold to count the empty barrels and sacks used for sugar and oranges but Jonathan thought he would go home early for tea in the hope that his grandfather's back had stopped hurting and that he had remembered his promise about going to see the rabbits playing.

"Right, Jonathan," said Mr Noah. "Ready after breakfast tomorrow for an early start."

"And bring your swimming costume and a pair of boots with you," said Mrs Noah. "Don't worry about pyjamas and such – Japhet has a spare pair you can borrow, and anything else you may need. Just swimming costume and boots is all you'll want."

Jonathan was so very excited at the idea of setting off on the voyage that he could not think of leaving the Ark behind in the attic. He picked it up and carried it home so that they could all set sail in the morning the moment breakfast was finished.

His grandfather was not in the garden, nor sitting in his chair reading the newspaper, but Jonathan heard voices upstairs. He went up and was shocked to see his grandfather flat on his back in bed looking very miserable, and his grandmother sitting in a chair beside the bed, talking to him.

"The awful thing is, this is just the sort of thing that could drag on for weeks and weeks, or even months," his grandfather was saying. "It makes me realise how beastly old I am, that's all."

"Oh, come now, John," his grandmother said. "Don't let's get too depressed before we know what it is. I'll just have to get the doctor to see you."

His grandfather made a face. "Doctor!" he said. "I hate doctors."

His grandmother looked up and saw Jonathan. "Hello, darling," she said. "Grandpa's back still hurts, so he decided he would go to bed to rest it properly."

Grandpa gave a sort of growl, to mean that it had been Granny who had done the deciding, not him.

"Sorry about your rabbits, Jonathan," he said. "I was looking forward to going with you but it looks as if we shall have to put it off."

Jonathan was disappointed about the rabbits, too, because he did very much want to see them dancing and playing. But it was much worse to see his grandfather, who was usually so lively and busy and cheerful, lying in bed looking ill and sad. He had said it could go on for weeks, or even months. Jonathan could not imagine it. His grandmother was very silent while they ate their tea, and he supposed she was worried too.

"Do you think the doctor will be able to make Grandpa get better?" asked Jonathan.

"Oh, I'm sure he will, darling," she said. "But poor Grandpa does so hate to have to stay lying still, doing nothing, and he might not be able to get up for a day or two."

Jonathan went to say good night to his grandfather before he went to bed.

"What are you going to do with yourself tomorrow?" asked his grandfather.

"I'm going for a voyage to the West Indies in the Ark, to get a cargo of sugar," said Jonathan happily, before he could stop himself. "If that's all right," he added rather anxiously, wondering if he was supposed to tell.

His grandfather smiled. "I shouldn't think there will be any objection," he said. "But are you sure it's safe to go all that way in the Ark?"

"Oh, the Ark's as safe as can be. Safer than houses, anyway, because they get flooded," said Jonathan.

His grandfather really laughed at that and looked happier than he had all day.

"You'd better get some sleep, then, before you start," he said. "Good night, Jonathan. Pleasant dreams!"

"Good night, Grandpa," said Jonathan. He hovered for a moment by the door, his hand on the knob.

"Grandpa," he said, "I'm glad you're old. Or at least, quite old."

His grandfather raised his eyebrows. "Oh?" he said. "Why is that?"

"Well, I don't think it would be much good having a grandfather who *wasn't* old," said Jonathan. "It would seem silly. And he wouldn't know everything if you wanted to ask about things."

This time Grandpa went on laughing for a long time and Granny came to hurry Jonathan off to bed, but she seemed pleased with him and gave him a very loving hug as she kissed him good night.

Jonathan lay down to go to sleep. Mrs Noah would probably know what to do about Grandpa's back, he thought. He must ask her in the morning. It must be getting quite late, though it was still light outside. The rabbits must be out by now. He fell asleep.

* * * *

Suddenly he was wide awake. There was a stamping and snorting down on the path behind the house under Jonathan's window, and a jingling of harness. The horse had come for him! Jonathan slipped out of bed and down to the back door. Upstairs, the faint murmur of his grandparents' voices did not stop as the bolt slid back, and outside the night air was friendly and still. Jonathan mounted the horse and they trotted quietly round the house and out into the lane, off to find a meadow where the rabbits were frisking and playing, hopping and somersaulting in the summer twilight.

7

Even by breakfast-time the next day the weather was very hot, and it seemed as though it was going to be the hottest day of the summer so far. Jonathan's grandmother had telephoned the doctor and he had promised to come and see Grandpa as soon as he could get away from his morning surgery. Granny had said that Jonathan could certainly go on a long voyage if that meant playing outside in the garden all morning, and agreed to let him wear his swimming costume and shirt. Yes, oh, yes, and his Wellington boots, too, if he thought he needed them!

Jonathan rushed upstairs to get changed. His grandfather was still in bed, lying flat and listening to the news on the wireless; it still hurt him to move the least bit, his grandmother said. Jonathan saw him lying there as he passed the door on his way to his own bedroom.

What could you do for grown-ups who were ill, he wondered. When he had been feeling very ill and miserable with measles, his mother had bought him a present, a toy car with doors that could open and shut. The car had made Jonathan feel much better but he could not think of anything to give his grandfather, even if he had any money to buy a present.

He had his swimming costume on now and looked round for his boots. Ah, there they were, at the back of the cupboard. He sat down on the floor and pulled them on, but ouch! What was this? Something hard was in the toe of one of his boots, digging into him. He pulled the boot off again, turned it upside down and shook it. Out fell a small star.

Jonathan gazed at it in amazement for a moment, wondering where it had come from. Of course, he had been wearing his boots when he went fishing that first time on the Ark. The star must have fallen into his boot. Jonathan picked it up and turned it over. It seemed to have gone hard, like a shell, and no longer throbbed and twinkled with light but it was still a star and a pretty, golden-yellow colour. Jonathan put his boot on again and went to see his grandfather.

"Hello, Grandpa," he said, coming to the side of the bed.

His grandfather was wearing his reading glasses and had the newspaper folded into a small square, so that he could hold it up to read.

"Oh, hello, Jonathan," said Grandpa in a tired voice. "Are you still going to the West Indies this morning?"

"Oh yes," said Jonathan happily. "We're just going off now, that's why I've got my boots on. Granny says I may go."

"Well, I'll see you when you get back," said his grandfather, "and you can tell me all about it."

"Yes," said Jonathan. He brought his hand from behind his back and held out the star to his grandfather.

"This is for you," he said. "It's a star, and I do wish your back would get better."

Jonathan's grandfather looked surprised. He laid down his newspaper and reached out for the star.

"It's a *what*?" he asked, and almost dropped the star as he took it from Jonathan. Without thinking he moved quickly to catch it, half sat up and said "Ouch!" very loudly indeed. Jonathan was horrified, but after staying in the same half-sitting position for a moment or two, while Jonathan held his breath, he seemed to relax and a pleased smile spread across his face.

"Well," said Grandpa happily, "Lord bless my soul!"

He sat right up in bed and took off his glasses.

"Do you know," he said, "it's stopped hurting. It must have been that jolt. Whatever was in the wrong place has gone back, I felt it. Good gracious me! Hey, Jonathan, go and tell your Granny I want her."

His grandmother came quickly up the stairs and found Grandpa sitting on the edge of the bed looking for his slippers.

"John, whatever is it? What are you doing, dear?" she said. "I'm sure you shouldn't be bending your back like that and you must get back into bed, the doctor will be here any minute to have a look at you."

"Then you'll be able to tell him to go away again," said Grandpa firmly. "I'm better. I felt something click back into place. Jonathan was just giving me a – where is it? Ah, yes, here on the bed. Good gracious, it's a starfish, a fossilised starfish. Wherever did you find this, Jonathan?"

"In my boot," said Jonathan. "I thought you might like it."

"You were right. I do like it," said his grandfather warmly. "I like it very much indeed. In fact, I can't remember a present I like more. Thank you, Jonathan. And now," he said, as he got to his feet, "don't let me keep you, if you're going to the West Indies. I'm going to get shaved."

Granny was laughing. "You certainly seem better," she said, "though I can't think what I shall tell the doctor when he comes. Perhaps a cup of coffee will turn away his wrath."

Grandpa turned back from the bathroom door. "Give him a cigar if you like," he said. "Look out for sharks, Jonathan!" and he disappeared into the bathroom to shave.

Granny was smiling to herself as she began to make the bed, and Grandpa could be heard whistling tunefully in the bathroom. Everything was all right again. Jonathan gave a great sigh of satisfaction, picked up the Ark from the head of the stairs and carried it outside into the sunshine.

8

The voyage started from the front lawn. The Ark simply sailed down the garden path, out onto the hot road and away until it came to the riverbank and slipped into the clear water. Once they were out on the river, where there was a light breeze blowing, it was cooler but there was not a cloud in the sky and everyone was in a joyful mood.

There were four bunks in the cabin, two on each side, with bright, patchwork bedcovers made by Mrs Noah. Jonathan shared the bar of chocolate his grandmother had given him with Japhet, and they arranged to take turns to sleep on the top bunk. Ham would sleep in the other top bunk and Shem in the one below, except when it was their turn to be on watch on deck. Mr and Mrs Noah had a cabin to themselves, next door.

Shem was at the wheel, and after talking to him for a while Jonathan and Japhet went to join Ham, who was leaning on the rail watching the water and the riverbanks slip past. The decks were clean and shining where they had been scrubbed in readiness for the voyage, and fluttering gaily from the stern was the Ark's own flag, a rainbow and a dove on a blue background. The river became larger and wider as they went on and other rivers or streams came tumbling into it. They began to meet other boats, rowing boats and river steamers and a little fleet of racing yachts with coloured sails. They went through locks and past the gardens of houses, many of them with their own boathouses at the edge of their green, sloping lawns. Then the buildings began to crowd closer to the riverside and the Ark went under big stone bridges. They passed tugs with strings of barges and a smart little River Police boat. Jonathan and Japhet waved and two policemen waved back.

"We're in London now," said Ham.

Mrs Noah came to join them and pointed out the different famous buildings as they passed. Big Ben and St Paul's Cathedral were the only two Jonathan really knew about but he liked the look of Cleopatra's Needle. The river bent slowly about, under London Bridge and past the Tower of London, and by a stroke of luck, just then a big Swedish ship going slowly downstream had to have Tower Bridge raised for it. All the buses and lorries and cars stood waiting at each side of the bridge while the two halves swung slowly up into the air, and the Ark sailed through too, rocking in the wake of the big ship.

"Ahoy, there, Ark!" called a voice from a ship whose cargo of timber was being unloaded with a crane. "Where are you bound?"

"West Indies," shouted back Mr Noah.

"Good voyage," called the man, "and a safe return!"

"Thank you, friend!" shouted Mr Noah.

They all waved until the man and his ship were out of sight, and the Ark sailed on, with Mr Noah at the wheel carefully finding a way through all the different kinds of ships and boats on the busy river, each with its name painted across the stern and its country's flag flying. Down past Greenwich and towards the sea they went. Mrs Noah called them in to lunch, and by the time it was cleared away and they came out on deck again, the river scenery had vanished.

"Salt sea water now, my boys," said Mr Noah, smiling contentedly.

That evening after supper, when Jonathan and Japhet were washed and in their pyjamas, Mr Noah took them out on deck. In the distance, far behind them, was a dark blue blur of land, with here and there a light twinkling and the regular flash of a lighthouse. In front, still stained pink by the sunset, nothing but sea. The voyage had really begun.

* * * *

They spent most of the next morning fishing over the stern with fishing lines.

"You can eat what you catch for your lunch," Mrs Noah said.

"Gosh!" said Jonathan. "Suppose we catch a whale!"

"Or a hammer-head shark!" said Japhet.

"Or an old boot!" said Ham teasingly, as he helped them to bait their hooks.

It was another hot day, and the boys had not bothered to put shirts on at all that morning. A few seagulls still flapped lazily behind the Ark, having followed them for a whole day. They were keeping a sharp eye open for any scraps and presently seemed very pleased with the bucket of potato peelings Shem carried out from the cabin and threw overboard. Jonathan and Japhet enjoyed watching them, screaming and diving to catch as much potato peel as possible before it sank through the green water, and Japhet very nearly lost his fishing-line before he noticed that he had actually hooked a fish.

An hour or so later, Ham, Japhet, and Jonathan had caught enough shining silver fish for everybody to eat for lunch, and Mrs Noah fried them most deliciously in butter. Ham said they were sardines, though Jonathan found it hard to believe that anything tasting so good could be related to tiny, oily sardines out of a tin, which he had never liked.

Sea air seemed to be very good for the appetite, and by the time they had finished eating, Jonathan and Japhet both felt rather heavy and slow and as if they should keep quiet and still for a while. But Mr Noah had other ideas and set them to work in the hold, sorting through the piles of empty sacks and looking for any with holes in them. These were put on one side and then carried up on deck to be mended. The huge doors into the hold were folded back to let the light and the fresh air in, and it looked just like a large barn.

Jonathan was surprised to find how heavy an empty sack could be. He and Japhet found it easiest to make several journeys to and fro, carrying only two torn sacks each time. They worked hard and sorted out all the sacks in need of mending, and Mr Noah was pleased with them. He sat on a wooden bench in the shade of the overhanging cabin roof, mending sacks and telling Jonathan stories of the Ark's voyages. Mrs Noah came and sat beside him, found herself a needle and began to help with the mending.

"You're a true farmer's lass," said Mr Noah to her. "Farmer's lass and farmer's wife – never idle."

Mrs Noah smiled at him and tossed the finished sack to Japhet to fold while she began another.

"But you're a sailor, Mr Noah, not a farmer," objected Jonathan. "Mrs Noah must be a sailor's wife."

"Ah, we were farmers once, before we built the Ark and took to the seafaring life, oh, yes, farmers born and bred," said Mr Noah tranquilly. "But that was years and years ago, past counting. That was – why, that was before the Flood," and he chuckled in his beard.

"What was the Flood really like, Mr Noah?" asked Jonathan. "Was it fun?"

"Fun? No, it wasn't fun," said Mr Noah consideringly. "It was, let me see, how shall I explain it to you? It was *worthwhile*. Satisfying. It was very hard work, a hard, hard job for us all, and a job we weren't accustomed to doing, in many ways. But when it was over and the job had been well done, then you had the happiness of knowing that you had been asked to do more than your best, and somehow you had done it."

"The hardest thing of all, if you ask me," said Mrs Noah, "apart from getting all those wet clothes to dry, was to keep two bored lions and two cross tigers and a pair of grumbling wolves, away from the sheep and goats and chickens. They nearly drove me silly, far worse than naughty children. You couldn't take your eyes off them for a moment."

"Whatever did you do?" asked Jonathan, fascinated.

"We kept them so overfed they could hardly move," said Mr Noah. "As soon as we noticed that some of the animals were restless and sly-looking, trying to slink down to the hold when our backs were turned, I realised it was the only thing to do. I set Shem and Ham to fishing, every single minute they could be spared, and the fish went to the animals with the hungriest look. You couldn't blame them. It wasn't in their nature to eat hay or raw carrots or fresh fruit."

"I can see Ham now," said Mrs Noah, "out there in the pouring rain with his hair so wet it looked as if it had been painted to his head, fishing and fishing. And the lioness lying there on the beam under the roof-edge, out of the wet, watching him with her great yellow eyes and waiting for more fish. One day, he and Shem got such a big catch between them that both tigers slept all day and all night, and didn't feel hungry even when they woke up. And the lions were as quiet and tame as pussycats for quite two days."

"No wonder Shem and Ham are good at fishing," said Jonathan, "after all that practice."

Mr Noah laughed. "Shem said, as we went ashore that first time, he said he would never touch a fishing line again in his whole life, his fingers were so blistered from fishing. But he enjoys it all right now, when it's only for ourselves. I must say, I enjoy sailing all the more myself now I don't need to worry about chimpanzees playing with my charts, or the mice moving house into the sacks of grain. Come to think of it, the elephants were probably the least bother of all, in spite of their weight. Nice, quiet beasts, elephants."

"And the birds were lovely," said Japhet. "I was allowed to climb up every morning and open the window, up in the roof, and they would all come flying out past me in a great cloud, hundreds and hundreds, twittering and singing, until I felt I could fly myself. The golden eagles would wait until last, and it was like the sun rising out of the window when they came out. The little birds would perch all over the place and chatter, and the big ones would disappear until just before dark when I went up to shut the window again."

"I'm glad you did take to the sea," said Jonathan. "And I'm glad I could come this time even if I did miss the Flood."

They sailed peacefully on across the sea through the sunny afternoon, pointing steadily westwards to where the sea and sky met, and it already seemed a long time ago, in another lifetime, that they had first begun the voyage.

Japhet and Jonathan went on helping Mr Noah in various ways. They rolled an empty water-barrel into the hold and into its proper place, though it took Shem and Mr Noah together to roll the full, heavy one back up the steep ramp along to the galley where Mrs Noah was taking a batch of hot loaves out of the oven. She baked bread every second day, and it was always crusty and mouth-watering. Japhet put out a hand to touch one loaf but it was still too hot to hold, let alone eat.

"Never mind," he said to Jonathan. "Not long before tea!"

"I never knew a boy like you for thinking of the next meal," said Mr Noah. "It doesn't seem five minutes since you were groaning you couldn't bend after your sardines. Look lively now! Come out from your mother's cooking, and I might let Jonathan take a turn at the wheel."

This idea was so exciting as to sound positively alarming to Jonathan, and his expression was anxious as he followed Mr Noah along the deck and took the wheel from Ham. He was surprised that the Ark did not capsize at once, or plunge straight to the bottom of the sea, but as it continued steadily on its course he began to enjoy the feeling of steering. He gripped the polished wooden spokes of the wheel less tightly and looked happier.

"That's better," said Ham. "When you came along, I thought from your face that Father was going to make you walk the plank."

The afternoon ended, the sun set, and Jonathan found that sea air, as well as being good for the appetite, was excellent for sending you to sleep. He was glad it was Japhet's turn for the top bunk because he felt almost too sleepy to climb the ladder.

"Good night, Japhet," he said, with a great yawn.

"Good night, Jonathan," said Japhet. "I wonder what you would have to put on a hook to catch a whale. Let's ask my father in the morning."

The Ark sailed on while the boys slept.

9

Each day followed another, very much to the same pattern as the last. Once they passed another ship (a cargo boat, Shem said), close enough to wave but for most of the time the whole sea seemed to belong to them. The weather became hotter and hotter and the boys folded up their warm, patchwork bedcovers, and put them away in a locker. They ate their midday meal on deck now, where the breeze kept them cool, and again, in the early evenings, they would find themselves a comfortable spot to sit in the stern, in the cool air, and sing. Mr Noah would stand at the wheel while Shem played his guitar and Ham joined in with his mouth-organ, and the whole crew would sing, starting with the loud, jolly songs, and ending with the slower, quieter ones. Jonathan's favourite was called 'The Voyaging Ark'. This song sometimes went on for a very long time, as it had dozens of verses, and sometimes Mr Noah would invent one or two more. Nobody minded if you got the words a bit muddled, as long as you sang your loudest and stayed on the note. They would sing all the verses they could remember, and then the chorus, very loudly, while everybody tried to remember some more. Then they would look hopefully at Mr Noah for a new one and then sing the chorus again, louder than ever. This is more or less how it went:

1. *Would you like to come sailing, away round the world,*
    On the Ark, the voyaging Ark?
The anchor's aweigh and the flag is unfurled,
    On the watertight, voyaging Ark.

2. *There's room for a toad, or a tortoise or two,*
    On the Ark, the voyaging Ark.
And if you ask nicely, we'll make room for you,
    On the valiant, voyaging Ark.

3. *The thunder's tremendous, the lightning's terrific,*
    Round the Ark, the voyaging Ark.
We've crossed the Atlantic, we'll cross the Pacific
    In our brave and unsinkable Ark.

Chorus

Oh, we've cheetahs and anteaters, badgers and bats,
    We've donkeys and monkeys and rabbits and rats,
    We've eagles and beagles and camels and cats,
        And we're off on our travels again.
    There are leopards and lions and lizards and llamas,
    The elephant's borrowed the rhino's pyjamas.
    We're all friends and thundery clouds don't alarm us,
        So come aboard out of the rain.

4. *All our four-footed friends are assured of our care*
    On the Ark, the voyaging Ark.
There's a place for the panda, a home for the hare,
    On the ever-hospitable Ark.

5. *On the rainiest days, we know what to do,*
    On the Ark, the voyaging Ark.
To keep them all happy by helping the crew,
    On the light-hearted, voyaging Ark.

6. *We issue them all with mops, buckets, and brooms,*
   On the Ark, the voyaging Ark.
With sweeping and scrubbing we banish the glooms
   From the ship-shape and glistening Ark.

Mr Noah

7. *Now Jonathan's with us, we're off and away*
   On the Ark, the voyaging Ark.
We've not heard such singing for many a day
   On the sun-warmed and star-sprinkled Ark.

Chorus

Oh, we've cheetahs and anteaters, badgers and bats,
   We've donkeys and monkeys and rabbits and rats,
   We've eagles and beagles and camels and cats,
      And we're off on our travels again.
   There are leopards and lions and lizards and llamas,
   The elephant's borrowed the rhino's pyjamas.
   We're all friends and thundery clouds don't alarm us,
      So come aboard out of the rain.

Jonathan particularly liked the part about the elephant and the rhino's pyjamas as by that time of the evening he was already wearing a pair of Japhet's. Time for singing was just before Jonathan and Japhet's bedtime, and when they had sung themselves hoarse and been packed off to their bunks by Mrs Noah, they could hear the chords of Shem's guitar still sounding out over the calm sea.

Once Jonathan dreamt he was playing with the Ark in his grandfather's garden. A car stopped at the gate and a man got out, humming to himself and swinging a small case. He said Hello to Jonathan, and his grandmother came to show him into the house. Jonathan went on playing and for some time he could hear talking and laughing and the sound of coffee cups. At last his grandfather and the man came out into the garden, still talking in the most friendly way.

"Hello, Jonathan, Doctor Hill likes your star," said Grandpa. "Are you tired of the West Indies yet? I hope you aren't burning in this sun."

"No, we haven't even got there yet," said Jonathan. "We're having a super time, and Mrs Noah has just put some cream on me so I won't burn."

"Has she, indeed? Good for Mrs Noah," said Grandpa, and he and Doctor Hill both laughed. "But I think Granny would like to put some more on, to make doubly sure, and there is a drink of orange juice waiting for you."

He walked on to the gate with the doctor, obviously a great friend already, and as Jonathan went to get his drink, he could hear Doctor Hill saying, "You must let me bring you along some cuttings, and I really would appreciate your advice about greenfly, if you could spare the time. Perhaps one afternoon…"

* * * *

They could tell the voyage was nearly over when they began to see flying fish. Jonathan had not been sure he believed in flying fish until the first time he saw one come soaring out of the clear water near the side of the Ark and splash glittering back. He rushed to fetch Japhet, and they hung over the rail half the morning, watching whole schools of flying fish nearby.

"Such pretty things, flying fish," said Mrs Noah, stopping

for a moment to watch too. "Like sea butterflies."

"They taste lovely, too," said Japhet.

Jonathan was horrified at the idea of eating such gorgeous creatures but when, several mornings later, they had grilled flying fish for breakfast, he had to agree that they were good.

"It does seem a pity to catch them, though," he said.

Shem smiled at him. "It's all right, Jonathan," he said. "Nobody caught them. They jumped aboard themselves. We found them on the deck early this morning."

At once, Jonathan felt much better about eating flying fish. He and Japhet took to getting up even earlier than usual in the cool of the early morning, and padding about on deck in their pyjamas, collecting the glittering fish in a flat, round basket.

"Not long before we reach the Sugar Island now, lads," said Mr Noah one morning, as he passed them on his way along the deck.

"How can you tell, Father?" asked Japhet.

Mr Noah smiled. "There are ways and ways of telling," he said. "Charts and calculations tell you. So do the birds."

"Birds? I haven't seen any birds for – oh, ages," said Japhet, looking up and around with his eyes screwed up against the sunshine. "Oh, gosh, yes! Look, Jonathan!" and he pointed to a line of sea-birds flying past.

"So, you see, we aren't far from land," said Mr Noah.

This was exciting news, and the boys kept a sharp look-out all day, longing to be the first to see the Sugar Island. They saw two ships during the morning and finally, soon after lunch, a sort of dark hump appeared over the horizon. Japhet called to

Mr Noah, who shaded his eyes with his hand and gazed ahead to where they were pointing.

"That's it, boys," he said. "Well done. That's Sugar Island."

Japhet and Jonathan danced about in glee and then rushed to the wheelhouse to tell Shem that land was in sight. He let Japhet take the wheel while he went to look, then came back smiling and whistling. Mrs Noah came to look too, and so did Ham, carrying the hammer and nails he had been using to mend a broken chair. The island seemed to stay as far away as ever for a long time but at last began to grow larger and more real as they sailed nearer, until just before sunset they could see the colours of the hills and the dusty green of the palm trees.

"Well, now, we'll lay to until morning," said Mr Noah, "and come in by daylight."

"What's 'lay to' mean?" said Jonathan quietly to Japhet.

"Stop sailing. Stay where we are," said Japhet, equally quietly back.

They all gazed over the sea towards the Sugar Island that evening as they were singing. The stars came out in the sky above them, as they did every night, but tonight there were also little friendly lights twinkling and shining along the shore as it grew dark.

The Ark began to sail again so early next morning that, by the time Jonathan and Japhet came on deck, they were close enough to the island to see hills and houses and trees and even the colours of the flowers. The water was so clear that they could see the seaweed and the sand at the bottom. A little way from the Ark it was a bright blue-green, like a picture of the sea in a gaily painted book, and further away, a deep navy blue. They sailed along the coast of the Sugar Island for a time, past a long, silver-white stretch of sand with palm trees and little pine trees growing behind it, round the tip of the island and past a whole line of little yachts bobbing at anchor. The boys were getting very hungry but the island and boats and the sea looked so fresh and new and exciting in the morning sunshine, that they could not bear to leave it all for breakfast inside. Japhet slipped away and came back with some fresh buttered rolls, which they ate as they leaned over the rail.

"When are we going to land, Shem?" asked Japhet, as Shem went whistling past.

"Not long now," answered Shem. "In the Sugar Island, you sail right up the river into the city. You moor there, right in the middle, and all the policemen and children and people going shopping, stop to look and smile and wish they were you."

This sounded far too glorious an idea ever to be true, especially on a real island with houses and hotels and roads and bicycles, but Shem was right. Mr Noah brought the Ark into the river mouth and upstream, past warehouses and banks and other buildings, into the city, where a great many boats were already moored. Mr Noah found a place at the side of the river between the bridge and a big schooner, and Ham and Shem moored the Ark. Japhet read the name of the schooner, 'Friendship Rose', painted on its bows.

"Good name for a boat," he said to Jonathan.

The road ran along so close to the river that you could lean down from the deck to shake hands with people passing on the pavement, and Mr Noah, smiling his friendly smile, had to go on doing so for some time. The Customs man who came aboard seemed delighted to see Mr Noah and laughed and joked with him like an old friend.

"Mr Noah seems to know a lot of people in the Sugar Island," said Jonathan.

"Oh, Father has friends everywhere, it's the same wherever we go," said Japhet happily. "I say, Jonathan, doesn't it feel funny, now we've stopped sailing?"

"Gosh, do your legs feel funny, too?" asked Jonathan. "I thought it was only me. I nearly fell over just now."

"No, everybody has it," said Japhet. "I bet even Shem is holding on to something."

The people of the Sugar Island were mostly brown-skinned, though there were also a great many pink people, all mixed in together. They all seemed very happy and friendly and in no time at all there was a group of people aboard the Ark, laughing, talking, and asking questions about the voyage. Shem and Ham had finished coiling ropes and tidying the decks, Mrs Noah had taken off her apron and smoothed her hair, and they all came to join in the talking and laughing. Three boys walking past over the bridge stopped to look down.

"Hey, there's Japhet," shouted one of them. "Hello! Coming swimming?"

Mrs Noah looked up. "That's right, boys," she said to Jonathan and Japhet, "you go along. Your costumes are dry in the cabin. Don't forget your towels."

Ham came too with several friends he had collected, and the whole group of them piled into a bus and swept off down the road to the silver-white beach they had sailed past in the Ark earlier that morning. As soon as they arrived, they all ran shouting and laughing into the water and dived and floated and swam. One of Ham's friends, Thomas, borrowed a surfboard from somebody he knew on the beach, and came riding in with the waves like an express train. It looked easy but when Jonathan and Japhet tried it themselves, they found that the board shot out from under them almost every time, and even when it did not they could not manage to stand up straight. At last they threw themselves onto the sand to dry in the sun.

"Oh," said Japhet blissfully. "I love voyaging but this is … oh, this is … "

Jonathan knew just what he meant. He rolled over on to his tummy and scooped up a handful of warm, silver sand.

"How long do you think we can stay on the Sugar Island?" he asked.

"Oh, I don't know, a few days," said Japhet. "I don't think Father means to rush, and there's the cargo of sugar to load up. Anyway, we'll be going on to the Spice Island next for Mother's spices, and that's another super place."

It was only after several more swims and races along the beach that they all collected up their towels and shoes, and went laughing and chattering through the little wood of pine trees to the main road. They climbed onto the bus to go back to Rivertown, and the bus-conductor laughed and joked with Ham as he paid the fares for all of them.

"How did you get the right sort of money, Ham?" asked Jonathan.

"I haven't got any money at all," said Ham. "I paid him with stars."

"Goodness, doesn't it matter?" said Jonathan.

"Matter?" repeated Ham, surprised. "No, he's delighted. Anybody would rather have stars than money, I should think."

It was quite hot on the bus, and everybody was getting hungry, so they were very glad when they reached Rivertown. Their friends hopped off at different stops and at last the bus brought them to the bridge nearest the Ark, and Ham, Japhet, and Jonathan climbed wearily aboard. It was delightfully cool and dim in the cabin. Mrs Noah had made them a great jug of cold fresh lime-juice and there was salad for lunch.

They spent four glorious days in the Sugar Island, swimming, surfing, sailing, and exploring. Mrs Noah bought new shirts for Mr Noah and the boys, and a shopping basket embroidered with bright blue raffia flowers for herself.

In the evenings, the Ark was never without several guests to supper, and they sang and danced until late, long past Japhet and Jonathan's usual bedtime.

On the last day, the boys helped to roll the barrels of sugar down the tailboard of the red lorry belonging to one of Mr Noah's friends, up the gangplank and down into the hold of the Ark. There were ten barrels of white sugar, four of brown, and three sacks of lump-sugar. Some sugar had been spilt in the back of the lorry, which was sticky and smelt mouth-wateringly of warm toffee. Shem had been to the warehouse the day before and said it was a huge place, like a barn with a corrugated iron roof, full of great mountains of sugar smelling sweeter than honey. Mr Noah and Ham tipped half a barrel of gleaming stars into the sack that Joe, the lorry-driver, held open, in payment for the sugar, and he swung it up into the cab of his lorry before coming back to see them off. They had also taken on board some coconuts and bananas, as well as two sacks of limes and some fresh vegetables, and all these things were stowed tidily in the hold.

Everybody they knew and many more people besides, came to stand on the bridge and wave them off. Many of them had brought presents, and Thomas arrived last of all at top speed on his bicycle, just as they were casting off, out of breath and with a present of a watermelon. Finally, the Ark swung round into the river and headed downstream to the sea, while the Noah family and Jonathan stood waving in the stern until the river bent away and their friends were hidden behind the buildings on the bank.

10

Sorry though they had all been to leave Sugar Island, it was good to be at sea again and voyaging on. It was not long, however, before there was a change in the perfect weather. It was still hot but unpleasantly airless. The cool breeze had dropped and it was sticky and uncomfortable, even quite early in the day. The sky was like a hot blue bowl turned upside down over the Ark, and the air was heavy and still.

"Something brewing up, I fancy," said Mr Noah, looking searchingly at the sky. "Best get a few windows shuttered, Shem. I'll take the wheel while Ham gives you a hand. And Japhet, get Mother's washing in, there's a good lad, before the wind comes."

Jonathan helped Japhet to unpeg the shirts hanging out to dry on the line stretched across the stern. It was so still, and he was wondering how Mr Noah knew that there was a wind coming when he felt the first puffs, like the hot breath of some enormous animal, on his face, and the sky began to turn a curious brownish colour.

"Gosh, Mother, I wish it would rain," said Japhet, as Mrs Noah met them at the cabin door. "It's just like when you open the door of the oven."

Mrs Noah took the washing from them and began to fold

the shirts. "I think it will rain all right," she said placidly, "and before very long. It's a mercy the furniture is mostly bolted to the floor. Your Father knew what he was about when he built the Ark."

Shem and Ham were going along the deck together, shutting and bolting the heavy wooden shutters over the windows until they were all done. Japhet and Jonathan went to make sure that all the lockers were properly fastened shut, so that fishing tackle and coils of rope would not spill out over the deck during the coming storm. The hot wind was blowing harder now and the fish had stopped jumping. There was a low grumble of thunder, far away, and the first huge drops of rain splashed down into the sea.

"Jonathan! Jonathan! It's a storm, come inside, darling!"

It was his grandmother's voice, and to his shock and immense disappointment Jonathan found himself kneeling in the grass in his grandfather's garden, with the Ark no more than a toy beside him. A few drops of rain fell and there was another clap of thunder, this time much nearer. Jonathan blinked, got to his feet in a daze and carried the Ark into the house.

"Goodness, Jonathan, you *were* in a dream," said his grandmother. "If I hadn't called you, you would have stayed out there in the rain and been soaked. Have you had a nice game?"

Jonathan felt like crying. This was too dreadful. He had so much wanted to be on the Ark in a storm, and now, just when the storm came, he had been called back. Japhet, Ham, and Shem, and Mr and Mrs Noah, all voyaging on without him – it was too much to bear.

"Oh, dear," he said, trying hard not to let the tears come, "it was going to be such a good storm too."

"Well, but darling, I couldn't let you stay outside in it," said his grandmother reasonably. "Why don't you watch it from your window-seat and pretend you're sailing in it."

"Yes, but how can I get back on the voyage, to where we were?" asked Jonathan in a miserable voice.

His grandmother looked at him helplessly but luckily his grandfather had been listening and came out into the hall.

"It's all right, Jonathan old chap," he said. "No need to be upset. You can find your way back, just as you can find your place again in a book. Just remember exactly what you were doing, what was happening, and off you go again."

Jonathan, his foot already on the bottom stair, looked at him hopefully.

"Do you really think so, Grandpa?" he said.

"Sure of it," said his grandfather positively. "Sure as eggs. Up you go now."

Jonathan went upstairs and put his Ark down on the window-seat. He felt chilly, and the rain was drumming on the roof and pouring down the windows. If only Grandpa was right. Remember exactly, he had said. Well, Japhet had been standing by the cabin door, and Shem and Ham were just ... There was a tremendous flash of lightning and a clap of thunder right overhead.

"Glory, that was a big one!" said Japhet. "Oh, Jonathan, you're back, thank goodness."

Jonathan stood in the pouring rain, smiling until his face ached.

"Oh, Japhet," he said, "was I gone long?"

"No, hardly at all," said Japhet loudly, over the noise of the wind and the rain. "Just long enough for me to wonder when you were coming back. Come on, let's go and ask Father what he wants us to do next. Hold on to the rail or you'll slip."

The storm was really upon them by now, and the Ark was rocking and plunging over huge waves, while the wind flung the rain in their faces and shrieked round the Ark. They battled their way along the deck to the wheelhouse, where it took both of them to tug the door open. As soon as it was open, the wind tore it away from them and crashed it back on its hinges while the charts began to flutter and fly like birds. Shem threw himself at the door and dragged it shut behind Jonathan and Japhet.

"Sorry, Father," said Japhet as they picked up the charts. "We came to ask what you wanted done."

Mr Noah went on fighting with the wheel without answering as they crashed through a wave and the Ark quivered along its whole length. Then he said, "Get two buckets from your mother and help Ham in the bows. Get rid of any water that comes over the side. Shem, lad, I want you to get a sea anchor out over the bows and come back here. If we can just keep her nose into the wind, we'll ride it out but it's a bad one all right."

This time, Shem managed the door for them, and Jonathan and Japhet slipped and fought their way along the deck to the cabin where Mrs Noah gave them each a bucket to use as a bailer. By now, it was very difficult to stand upright at all as the deck was tilting wildly under their feet but they clung to the door frame until the Ark steadied, then made another dash for the rail. The lightning seemed to split the sky right overhead, the thunder crashed about their ears, and the rain was coming down faster than ever, hissing into the angry sea.

Ham was braced against the front wall of the cabin, facing into the bows, a bucket between his feet. Jonathan and Japhet went to lean beside him, swaying with the Ark as it rolled, and watching Shem setting the sea anchor over the bows. He had no sooner finished and gone aft again than a huge green wave broke over the Ark, and the water came swilling past them up to the tops of their boots. They waited until the first force of it had gone, then began to scoop the water up in their buckets and throw it back over the side into the sea as fast as they could. Jonathan started by filling his bucket to the brim but quickly found that it was much too heavy to lift properly, so he scooped a little at a time to throw overboard and saw that Ham and Japhet were doing the same. Another wave hit them, though they shipped less water this time, then another very big one.

There was water inside both Jonathan's boots now, making it even harder not to fall over as he moved about the deck, but they had been given a job to do and he was not going to give up, though the mountains of water seemed sure to win against the three buckets. 'Better than your best', Mr Noah had said you sometimes had to do on the Ark, and Jonathan was part of its crew now. Ham, Japhet, and he clung grimly on each time the Ark hit a wave, and scooped up water as hard as they could when it had gone. They were all three soaked to the skin and running with water, their boots squelching at every step. It was quite impossible to talk because of the noise of the wind and the rain and the sea but they kept hard at work until their arms ached and they had lost all count of time.

Once, Japhet was caught off balance as the Ark lurched sideways, and went flying across the deck as if he meant to do a running dive into the sea but Ham dropped his bucket and threw himself in the way just in time. Both he and Japhet fell in a heap on the deck and were half drowned by the next wave pouring in over the side. Jonathan clung to the rail, unable to do anything to help but they seemed to be all right and staggered to their feet again as the Ark righted itself.

After a long time, Jonathan realised that the thunder and lightning and the rain had stopped. The waves were still enormous and threatening but the wind had stopped trying to tear the roof off the Ark and had dropped to a stiff breeze. The sun was already beginning to shine again. The storm was over.

Without a word, the three of them went wearily back along the swaying deck, almost too tired to carry their empty buckets. They left their boots in a pile by the door and nearly fell into the cabin.

"Come on, boys, well done," said Mrs Noah. "There's hot soup ready for you but first get all those wet clothes off. I've put dry things out for you on your bunks, and these towels are warm, so off you go. Don't go dripping wet trousers over your beds, now," and Mrs Noah turned back to the stove to stir the soup. The she went outside on deck to open one of the shutters and let some light into the cabin.

Ham, Japhet, and Jonathan climbed out of their wet clothes, dried themselves and rubbed hard at their hair. It felt wonderful to put on clean, dry clothes, and by the time they were dressed again, they were more than ready for soup. They sat round the table and had begun to eat, in a companionable silence, when Shem came in, having opened the rest of the shutters. He was not perhaps quite as wet as they had been but his shirt was soaked and he looked very tired. He went to change his shirt and came over to the table for his soup.

"That was quite something, wasn't it, Mother?" he said, and could not stop a guilty, pleased smile spreading across his face as he began to spoon up his soup.

"Look at you," said Mrs Noah. "Just like your father. Nothing you like better, any of you, than a really good storm. Well, we've all missed our lunch so there's soup now and an early supper."

"Missed lunch? Whatever is the time?" asked Ham. "It can't have been more than eleven o'clock when the storm started."

"It's nearly a quarter to five now," said Mrs Noah, "and supper will be at half-past six."

The boys looked at each other in amazement. Just imagine, the whole day disappearing without their noticing! They had been too busy even to feel hungry, though the soup was just what they wanted now. When it was finished, Jonathan and Japhet collected all the wet clothes for Mrs Noah in one of the buckets they had used for bailing, and Ham went to prop their boots upside down in a corner of the deck to dry. When he reappeared in the doorway of the cabin he was smiling.

"Come and look," he said. "There's a rainbow."

With one accord, everybody stopped what they were doing and went outside. The sea was already blue and sparkling again, and the wet decks steamed in the sun. Ham pointed, and there, some way ahead of the Ark, was a beautiful rainbow arching over the sea.

"Oh, what a beauty!" exclaimed Mrs Noah. "It looks as if the Ark will sail right under it. Shem, go and tell your father."

Mr Noah came along the deck, having given the wheel to Shem, and stood in the bows without a word. He did not smile or speak but stood very still, gazing at the rainbow with a calm, happy expression on his face. Mrs Noah slipped away to the cabin to pour out the soup she had kept hot for him, Ham went to talk to Shem at the wheel, and Jonathan and Japhet kept very quiet and still. Mr Noah went on looking at the rainbow. Jonathan had not noticed before how much Mr Noah looked like Mr Nelson. They might even have been taken for brothers. At last, the rainbow faded and Mr Noah went to eat his soup.

Ham went to see whether any of the cargo had shifted while the Ark was pitching and tossing during the storm but all was well, apart from two empty barrels, which had fallen over and were rolling about loose. Jonathan and Japhet helped him put them to rights, then came back to lean side by side on the rail.

"Good storm, wasn't it?" said Japhet.

"Super," said Jonathan. "It was dreadful, though, when I thought I couldn't get back."

"I know," said Japhet. "But I knew you'd manage."

They went on leaning on the rail until Mrs Noah called them in to supper, and as soon as supper was over they crawled gratefully into their bunks and fell asleep.

* * * *

They sailed on towards the Spice Island. The sea was again friendly and calm, the flying fish came aboard in time for breakfast, and the crew members of the Ark were burnt browner and browner by the sun. The Spice Island was sighted early one morning by Mrs Noah, on her way to peg sheets on the line, and by mid-afternoon they were anchored off the shore.

The very special thing about the Spice Island was its smell. While the Ark was still sailing towards the island, the breeze carried to them a marvellous scent of the spices growing ashore. Jonathan thought at first he had imagined it and took another, deeper breath.

"Ah, Jonathan," said Mr Noah, "you're smelling the spices already. That's one of the wonders of the world, the perfumed winds blowing across the blue sea from this island. I've sailed here more times than a few but to me it's still almost past belief."

He knocked the ashes out of his pipe over the side of the Ark and put it away in his pocket, and Jonathan noticed that he did not light it again until, two days later, they had sailed away from the Spice Island and left it far behind.

The Spice Island was smaller and quieter than the Sugar Island but a very pretty place. The Ark lay at anchor in the clear water, and the other members of the crew swam and basked in the sunshine while Mrs Noah went happily off to town with her basket to meet and talk with old friends in the market as she shopped for her packets of spices.

On the dresser in the cabin stood Mrs Noah's spice chest. It was beautifully made of polished wood, like a miniature chest of drawers, or tall-boy, with a little mirror at the top. As she cooked, Mrs Noah would open a particular drawer to take a pinch of this or a grain of that, a stick of cinnamon, or a bay leaf, a few peppercorns, or some rosemary leaves, to add flavour to whatever was bubbling on the stove. When she had bought her new stock, she emptied and cleaned the drawers, one at a time, and filled them with the pungent fresh spice. Ham gave her a hug.

"You do love to stock up, Mother, don't you?" he said. "You're wearing your special, satisfied look that means you're thinking of all the good flavours you'll put in the next stew."

"More power to your elbow, lass," said Mr Noah. "I've never yet tasted cooking to compare with yours."

Mrs Noah laughed but looked even more pleased than before, and the lunch she served a little later would have delighted a prince. It certainly delighted the crew of the Ark and they lay sprawled on the deck for some time afterwards, feeling far too heavy to risk diving into the water. They watched the pelicans, gliding gracefully in a line across the water, their heads turning from side to side as they searched for fish. Suddenly, they would fall into the water in an ungainly heap as if they had been shot, only to come up again with a fish in their beaks and continue their smooth flight as if nothing had happened.

"They look so beautiful while they are flying," said Mrs Noah, who was sitting in the shade, her hands, for once, resting in her lap. "But they dive so clumsily they look quite ugly."

"You watch them come into land on that coconut palm to eat their fish," said Shem. "Look at that – feet first, looking ridiculous. They are just like old ladies on bicycles with their feet off the pedals, terrified they aren't going to be able to stop for the traffic lights when they reach the bottom of the hill."

It described the pelicans so exactly that the crew of the Ark rolled about on the deck, laughing and wiping their eyes, and even Mr Noah could not stop chuckling. The nearest pelican gave Shem a dignified, injured look and flapped away to fish in the next bay.

The following morning, after taking on fresh water, they set sail for home. The weather was mostly good, though they did have some heavy rain, and it grew gradually cooler as they sailed on.

"I haven't seen a single shark the whole time," said Jonathan to Shem.

"No, they stay well clear of the Ark," said Shem, "and a good thing, too."

At last, one day Mr Noah called Jonathan into the wheelhouse as he was on his way to look for Japhet, and beckoned him over to look at the chart. Each day at sundown Mr Noah looked at the sun and the horizon with his sextant, and worked out where they were. He made a little cross on the map each time, and now the line of crosses stretched all the way to the West Indies and back again.

"You see, Jonathan," Mr Noah was saying, "we should soon be able to sight the coast of Spain ... " when faint and far away Jonathan heard his grandmother's voice calling him to lunch.

"I think I'll have to go, Mr Noah," he said.

"That's right, Jonathan, don't keep them waiting," said Mr Noah. "I'll tell Japhet where you are and we'll look to see you when we've taken on our oranges."

"Jonathan! Come on, darling!"

"I'm on my way, Granny, just coming," answered Jonathan, and with a rush and a blur he was back, kneeling on the window-seat in his bedroom. He looked down at the Ark and knew it was voyaging in Spanish waters with all the Noah family safely on board. He gave a satisfied sigh and went downstairs to have his lunch.

11

The kitchen was full of sunshine and the smell of fish and chips. Jonathan's grandfather smiled at him as he sat down. "Well," he said, "had a good voyage?"

"Yes, thank you, Grandpa, very good," said Jonathan, pulling his chair in closer to the table. "You were clever to know how to get back in the storm. It worked beautifully."

His grandfather cleared his throat modestly. "Glad to be of help," he said.

"I must say, you have gone beautifully brown, Jonathan," said his grandmother, as she passed his plate. "You're looking really well again."

"Nothing like a sea-voyage to set a fellow up," said his grandfather. "All that fresh air. I'm sure your mother will notice a big improvement in you. By the way, dear, shouldn't we have heard from them by now about the holiday?"

"Good gracious, John, yes, you're quite right," said his grandmother. "With your back and the doctor coming and everything, I had quite forgotten today was Friday. Susan was going to let me know today whether everybody was well enough to go to the seaside. I do hope the girls are getting over measles all right. Still, I expect everything has been very difficult and nobody has had time to write letters."

Lunch was barely cleared away, however, when the doorbell rang. Jonathan opened the door to a tall lady dressed for riding and holding a letter.

"Hello, is your grandmother about?" she asked him.

"Yes, she's just coming – gosh! Is that your horse?" said Jonathan, startled, as he caught sight of a large horse tethered to the gate.

"Yes, that's Highboy," said the lady. "He's got very good manners. You can go and talk to him if you like."

Jonathan went to look at the horse while the visitor was explaining to his grandmother that she had had a letter delivered to her by mistake and thought it must belong here. No, she would not come in now, thank you, but she would like to call properly sometime soon. She went back down the path, untethered Highboy, sprang lightly into the saddle, which seemed to be several miles from the ground, and with a wave to Jonathan trotted off down the lane.

"What a nice person," said Jonathan's grandmother. "Look, Jonathan, she's brought a letter from Daddy. Let's go inside and see what it says."

Jonathan hopped about impatiently while his grandmother found her glasses and ran her eye down the letter. It seemed a very long time indeed since he had come away from home, and all in a rush he began to think about his mother and father and the others. His grandmother looked up and smiled at Jonathan.

"There now, everybody's better," she said. "Isn't that good news? Daddy says you will be going to the seaside after all and he will collect you from here on the way to Cornwall, early on – let me see now – Saturday morning. But goodness me, Saturday is tomorrow. John! John, dear, where are you? The letter has come," and she hurried off to show the letter to Grandpa.

Tomorrow! Tomorrow morning, early, they would collect him! Jonathan thought he would burst with excitement and happiness. They would go to the sea and swim and make sandcastles and eat that special sort of ice cream, and Daddy would be on holiday with them all the time instead of going to work, and Mummy would feel happy and make them all laugh and, oh, everything was going to be perfect. Jonathan rushed into the kitchen to find his grandmother and ask her if he could start packing. She looked at his happy face and laughed.

"Well, darling, don't start actually packing yet," she said, "but you could collect some of your things together. Your boots are by the back door and there seem to be quite a lot of marbles about – at least three in the bathroom. It would be a great help if you could take them all upstairs and anything else of yours you come across. We promised to go to tea with Mrs Nelson this afternoon and I'll pack for you when we get back."

"You'll have to be in bed early if you're going to be ready when Mummy and Daddy arrive to fetch you," put in his grandfather. "I expect the girls are looking forward to seeing you too, they must have missed you."

Jonathan felt that, although he had not realised it before, he also had been missing his family most dreadfully and he did not know how he was going to wait until the morning to see them. It was a good thing he was invited out with his grandmother to tea with Mrs Nelson because it gave him something to do besides waiting for bedtime. It was only when he had changed into a clean shirt and shorts and was ready to go that he suddenly caught sight of the Ark on the window-seat.

"Goodness, Granny, the Ark, I nearly forgot," he said in horror.

"Oh, yes, Jonathan, how lucky you remembered it," said his grandmother. "We must take it back to Mrs Nelson. Come on, darling, it's time to go."

Jonathan picked up the Ark with a rather thoughtful expression. In the excitement of thinking about his family he had not thought about saying goodbye to the Noah family, to Japhet especially. As he went through the gate and down the lane towards the vicarage, walking between his grandfather and grandmother, he wondered how the voyage was going and whether they had taken on the oranges and were making for home. The thing to do, decided Jonathan, was to take the Ark up to the attic himself. This would at least give him chance to go on board the Ark one last time to say goodbye.

Mr and Mrs Nelson were sitting in the shade of a large copper-beech tree, and came to welcome them at the gate.

"It's so lovely outside since the storm," said Mrs Nelson. "Would you like to have tea out here in the garden, or would you rather be inside?"

"Oh, I'd love to sit in your garden if it doesn't make tea a problem," said Granny. "The storm has cleared the air – I found it almost unbearably hot this morning."

"Well, now, Jonathan, we shall need a stool for you to sit on," said Mrs Nelson. "If you will make yourselves comfortable out here, Jonathan and I will go to find a stool and make some tea. Come along inside, my dear, I think the kettle must be boiling already."

Jonathan went with Mrs Nelson into the house and she was very interested to hear that he was going to Cornwall the next day. As they passed the stairs on their way to the kitchen he put down the Ark, which was getting very heavy, promising himself to take it up to the attic after tea. The white cat was sitting on the kitchen window-sill, smelling a bowl of roses but jumped down and let Jonathan stroke his head before going out into the garden.

"What is your cat's name?" asked Jonathan.

"Sohrab," said Mrs Nelson, busy with the teapot. "It's a Persian name because he's a Persian cat. He seems to like you, Jonathan. He won't usually allow visitors to stroke him, he just goes away. He's very independent." She put the teapot on the tray with the cups and saucers. "Now, if you can manage the milk jug," she said, "I'll bring this tray, and we can come back for the other tray and your stool."

Having tea in the garden was lovely, particularly as Mrs Nelson was not the sort of person to ask you to tea and give you nothing to eat. Jonathan had sometimes been with his mother to tea parties which were mostly conversation, then when you went home afterwards you had to have another, real tea before going to bed. This was a proper tea party with tomato sandwiches, egg sandwiches, biscuits, little cakes, and a delicious chocolate sponge with really thick chocolate icing. His grandfather said it was his favourite kind of cake, and had two slices.

After tea, Mr Nelson took Grandpa off to look at the roses and Jonathan went with Mrs Nelson and his grandmother to look round the garden. He had thought he knew the garden quite well but Mrs Nelson showed him a little ornamental pond with waterlilies in it that he had never seen before, and a sundial on the wall of the house. It was time to go home before he remembered the Ark.

"Gosh, Mrs Nelson, the Ark! I haven't taken it up to the attic," he said when they were already all saying goodbye to one another at the gate.

"That's all right, my dear, don't worry," said Mrs Nelson. "I'll take it up."

"Couldn't I go now?" asked Jonathan. "I'd be very quick."

"No, Jonathan, don't go and disappear now," said his grandmother. "Remember you have to be in bed early tonight so that you aren't still asleep when Daddy comes. Say goodbye to Mrs Nelson, and we must go."

"Goodbye, Mrs Nelson," said Jonathan. "Thank you for letting me play in your attic. I liked it very much, and all the toys, especially the Ark. I hope David won't mind that I borrowed it."

"How nice of you to remember that the Ark was David's," said Mrs Nelson, surprised and pleased. "I'm sure he'll be very pleased when I tell him you have enjoyed playing with it. You must come again to play, whenever your grandmother can spare you."

Jonathan said goodbye to Mr Nelson and walked home again with his grandparents, too busy talking about going to Cornwall to think sad thoughts about the Ark. But when he was in bed and his grandmother had packed his suitcase, tucked him in and gone downstairs, Jonathan sat up, hugging his knees and thinking it all over.

It had been a brilliant holiday. Mrs Nelson was nice, and Lukey, and the attic was super, full of adventures. Then the Ark. Oh, the Ark. It was as safe and familiar as your own bed, yet as exciting as your wildest dreams. Jonathan would never forget it. When he came to stay with his grandmother again he would go straight to see Japhet. Japhet must know that Jonathan would not have gone away without saying goodbye if he could help it. Jonathan hoped so anyway. At least Japhet was aboard the Ark, not left in the doll's house, alone with a pack of silly dolls. Jonathan thought of the Ark as he had last seen it, a little toy boat on the bottom stair in the vicarage hall, with Japhet one of five painted figures rattling inside, and he could not help minding rather. But tomorrow he would see his father and mother and the others and they would go to the seaside. Jonathan sighed softly and lay down.

When a hand shook his shoulder and he heard Japhet's voice in his ear, he thought he was dreaming of his bunk in the Ark and turned over, muttering sleepily. Then Japhet laughed, and he sat bolt upright in bed, very wide awake indeed.

"Oh Japhet!" he said joyfully. "I didn't even say goodbye."

"I should think not," said Japhet, laughing. "Come on, look lively, never mind your boots."

"Just as well," said Jonathan. "They're packed right at the bottom."

The Ark bobbed on the landing in its pool of moonlight as it had done once before, and Jonathan hurled himself happily up the gangplank with Japhet hard on his heels. Ham gave him a friendly slap on the shoulder.

"Father wants to talk to you so that he can mark your house on his chart straight away," he said, "and this holiday place, too. Then we're off fishing again."

Jonathan and Japhet went off together along the deck as the Ark rose towards the window, Jonathan feeling quite giddy with happiness. On their way to see Mr Noah in the wheelhouse they passed the open cabin door out of which was coming the most wonderful smell. Mrs Noah was making marmalade.

Printed by: Copytech (UK) Limited trading as
Printondemand-worldwide.com
9 Culley Court, Bakewell Road, Orton Southgate,
Peterborough, PE2 6XD